Praise for TONY BLACK

'Tony Black is my favourite British crime writer.'
                    Irvine Welsh, author of *Trainspotting*

'Tony Black is one of those excellent perpetrators of Scottish noir ...
a compelling and convincing portrayer of raw emotions in a vicious
milieu.'
                                                        The Times

'If you're a fan of Ian Rankin, Denise Mina and Irvine Welsh this is
most certainly one for you.'
                                                    The Scotsman

'Black renders his nicotine-stained domain in a hardboiled slang that
fizzles with vicious verisimilitude.'
                                                    The Guardian

'Ripping, gutsy prose and a witty wreck of a protagonist makes this
another exceptionally compelling, bright and even original thriller.'
                                                    The Mirror

'This up-and-coming crime writer isn't portraying the Edinburgh in
the Visit Scotland tourism ads.'
                                                        The Sun

'Comparisons with Rebus will be obvious. But that would be too
easy ... Black has put his defiant, kick-ass stamp on his leading man,
creating a character that deftly carries the story through every razor-
sharp twist and harrowing turn.'
                                                    Daily Record

'At the front of the Tartan Noir pack ... a superior offering in an
already crowded Scottish crime market.'
                                                    The Big Issue

'Black really excels with his depiction of Edinburgh's low-life scum
... an accomplished and impressive piece of Tartan Noir.'   *The List*

'An authentic yet unique voice, Tony Black shows why he is leading
the pack in British crime fiction today. Atmospherically driven, the
taut and sparse prose is as near to the bone you are ever likely to
encounter in crime noir. Powerful.'
                                        New York Journal of Books

'Tony Black is the Tom Waits of Crime fiction, yes, that good.'
                    Ken Bruen, author of *London Boulevard*

'With comparisons to the likes of Irvine Welsh and William
McIlvanney echoing in his ears, Tony Black has become a top-class
author in his own right.'
                                                    3AM Magazine

'One of the strongest voices in the UK crime scene at the moment, and it's a voice that gets clearer and more precise with each book. Tony writes with blunt force, creating dark and brutal stories that still manage to crack a gallus smile.'
Do Some Damage

'You want something even more refreshing than a pint or two of the black stuff? Then give Tony Black's stuff a go.'
Crime Scene Northern Ireland

'The humour amid the pain is brilliant and should have broad-minded readers rocking in their chairs ... a compelling new crime novelist.'
Suite.101

'Sharp pacing and with a wonderful narrative, Black delivers a book that can't be put down and will stick with you after reading. If this were Nascar, Black would be holding a lot of chequered flags.'
Crimespree

'Tony Black, take a bow. This first-person narrative is a super-charged, testosterone-filled force of nature and I defy anyone not to get caught up in it ... a rollercoaster ride from riveting start to exhilarating finish.'
Crime Squad

'Wonderfully written, tough, edgy, and very dark, but with the odd flash of humour. Tony Black is a brilliant writer.'
Big Beat from Badsville

'Powerful, focused, and intense ... and then it gets better. Get your money down early on this young man – he's dead serious and deadly accurate.'
Andrew Vachss, author of *Hard Candy*

'Tony Black is already one of my favourite living crime writers.'
Nick Stone, author of *Mr Clarinet*

'This is pure noir, sublime and dark as a double dram of Loch Dhu.'
Craig McDonald, author of *Head Games*

'If you haven't read Black, you're missing out on one of the best new voices to emerge from Scotland in the last few years. One of the best new voices to enter the genre, period.'
Russel D. McLean, author of *The Lost Sister*

'Black is the new noir.'
Allan Guthrie, author of *Two-Way Split*

The Storm Without, A Doug Michie Crime Thriller
Published by McNidder & Grace

Still recovering from the harrowing case that ended his police career, Doug Michie returns to his boyhood home of Ayr on Scotland's wind-scarred west coast. He hopes to rebuild his shattered life, get over the recent failure of his marriage and shed his demons, but the years have changed the birthplace of the poet Robert Burns.

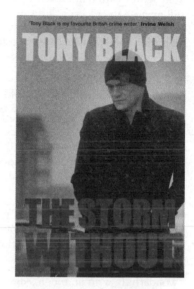

When Doug meets his old school flame Lyn, however, he feels his past may offer the salvation of a future. Soon Doug is tangled in a complicated web of corrupt politicians, frightened journalists and a police force in cahoots with criminals. Only Burns' philosophical musings offer Doug some shelter as he wanders the streets of Auld Ayr battling *The Storm Without*. ISBN 9780857160409.

'This is an elegiac noir for the memory of a place, delivered in prose as bleakly beautiful as the setting.' *THE GUARDIAN*

'This is the Great Scottish Novel, got it all and just a wee shade more... Classic.' KEN BRUEN, author of *HEADSTONE*

'Another master class in Tartan Noir.' *DAILY RECORD*

Also by McNidder & Grace is Tony Black's acclaimed *Last Orders*, an anthology of Short Stories which features the return of reluctant Edinburgh investigator Gus Dury in *Last Orders* and *Long Way Down*.

'Ripping, gutsy prose...makes this exceptionally compelling, bright and original.' *THE MIRROR*

For Jimmy 'the Piper' Murray

TONY BLACK

THE INGLORIOUS DEAD

MᶜNIDDER | & GRACE

Published by McNidder & Grace
Bridge Innovation Centre,
Pembrokeshire Science and Technology Park,
Pembroke Dock SA72 6UN

www.mcnidderandgrace.co.uk

First Published in 2014

A catalogue record for this work is available from the British
Library.

ISBN: 9780857160461

Designed by Obsidian Design

Printed and bound in the United Kingdom by
Latimer Trend & Company Limited, Plymouth.

Acknowledgements

So many people have helped make the publication of this book a lot easier than it should have been and I'd like to thank – in no particular order and with apologies to those I've left out unintentionally – Cheryl McEvoy, first reader, serial editor and all-round lovely person: huge thanks for everything, Chez! Julie Lewthwaite, thanks for an outstanding editing job, and sparing my blushes, not for the first time. Michael Malone, a big thank you for that all-important read through, and copious coffees at Su Casa. And, as always, thanks to my beloved and precious wife Cheryl for allowing me to write a book when we had a one-year-old in the house.

Till fate shall snap the brittle thread;
Then, all unknown,
I'll lay me with th' inglorious dead
Forgot and gone!

Robert Burns,
Epistle to James Smith

Chapter 1

It was like watching an old clock wind down, or the battery in a child's toy car cough the last few revolutions of energy to the wheels. Time froze, or at least, that's how it felt. You watched the slow-motion demise with a kind of detached uncertainty, a disbelief almost; not just for what you were seeing, but for the fact that so much time had passed before this point. Where had the years went? The long days of summer and the longer nights of cold winter when the dog curled himself in a black ball before the fire and shivered with each shrill blast breaking beneath the door.

I stroked his back but he remained motionless. Ben was silent now, as he was most days. He didn't bark like he used to, get enraged at a passer-by on the path beyond the garden or a rattle of the letterbox. He slept soundly most of the day, occasionally dragging himself towards the water bowl or the back door. I kept the door open for him, let him trail into the garden and seek out the odd oblong of sunlight where he'd lie down on the grass. He was totally blind but could always find the warmest patch. Was it habit? Instinct?

His instincts were telling him something else, too; in his own mute way he was informing me what he knew for sure. I'd tried to ignore him when he put his milky-white eyes on me and started the stertorous gasps for breath, but I'd never been very good at wilful ignorance. Facts were facts and didn't cease to exist because they were ignored, or so I'd heard on the force.

'So, that's that, Ben ...'

The dog barely raised a stiff grey eyelid at the sounding of his name. His heavy breathing bothered him, his tongue lolling on the side of his mouth.

'Come on, boy.'

There didn't seem any point to the pretence of attaching the lead, but I afforded him that dignity. He managed to walk all the way from the kitchen to the front door before his legs swayed beneath him, then he lay down and put his head upon his paws.

I eased onto my haunches and set a hand on his head; there wasn't a flicker of recognition. I carried him the rest of the way to the car and placed him on the back seat.

'Good boy.' The words of solace were more for me than him – his hearing had recently went from selective to non-existent. I felt a dig of conscience for having prolonged his misery for so long.

On the way along the Maybole Road towards the veterinary practice, I tried to clear my mind; opened the window and let a little of the warm sun insinuate itself on my skin. It seemed too nice a day for the task at hand; on sunny days the Ayrshire coast came alive within the sparkling seas. Such a rarity was not to be missed, but I knew I'd remember this day for all the wrong reasons.

The Audi's dash lit up; it was my mobile phone ringing through the blue-tooth connection. I pressed the 'receive call' button.

'Hello ...'

'Alright, Doug. How you doing there, mate?'

It was a voice I recognised, another *mate* I'd collected – or should that be an old mate I'd reconnected with – during my year of settling back into the old home town. It was strange how the decades of distance seemed to account for nothing, a brief retelling was all that was needed before the reminiscences of times gone by covered over the gaps.

'Andy, how's yourself?'

'Och, mair to fiddling ... you know the score.'

That I did. The score had, if it was possible, settled into negative figures for my old friend. I tried to tip my voice into the vicinity of hale fellow well met, but it was a battle. I eyed the motionless dog on the backseat as I spoke, 'Look, I'm driving, Andy, what can I do you for?'

'Driving, on the hands-free, I hope?'

'Aye, taking the dog to the vet ...'

'Oh, I see ... the time's come then?'

I'd filled Andy in on my current quandary with the dog. 'I think so.'

Andy reversed the roles, tried to play the chipper hand; I didn't think he knew it was in the pack. 'Well, you'll be needing a pint after a job like that, Doug ...'

He wasn't wrong. I'd been trying to cut back on my drinking of late, reducing the intake to a couple of nights a week. Too many of my mates, like Andy, seemed to restrict themselves to only on days with a 'y' in.

'I don't know, I mean ...'

Andy cut me off, his tone shifted into an area that was all new to me. 'Oh, come on ... you know I'm right. It's on me, as well.'

Andy never stood his round, and his luck at the bookies was all one way.

'Is everything okay, pal?' I said.

'Okay ... Christ, aye. Never been better.'

He was overdoing it, protesting too much. My curiosity dial went up to eleven.

'Okay, give me an hour, and I'll see you in Billy Bridge's.'

'Smashing, mate ... see you there.'

The line died.

As I was pulling into the vets, negotiating the pot-holed car park, I sought out a space as close to the front door as I could. I knew I'd have to carry Ben in there.

I stilled the engine and removed the key from the ignition. As I turned towards the old dog, the shift of his breath was barely audible, his greying flank rising almost imperceptibly.

I felt my throat constricting as I turned away and opened the car door.

The sun was warm on my face but my heart was cold in my chest.

'Here we are now, Ben.'

Chapter 2

Ben barely acknowledged the long needle; it went in without any struggle. I remembered him as a pup, his first injections, and the trouble I'd had stopping him from rearing up on the vet's table. Those days seemed a million years ago. There was no struggle now, just a slow release from the pains of existence. The dog lay there, his life's force spent; I tried to pat his head, ruffle his ears, but there was no reaction. He was gone. There was nothing left of the old Ben I once knew.

I walked from the small surgery towards the front counter and fumbled for my wallet. More people had arrived now, the busy time of the evening starting up.

'It's okay,' said the receptionist.

Her words confused me. 'Sorry?'

'There's nothing to pay just now ... we'll take care of the arrangements and let you know.'

I returned my wallet to the inside of my jacket and headed for the door. I didn't think I had even thanked them for their kindness.

In the car I sat with the window open and lit a Marlboro. I hadn't noticed my hands were shaking, or the cigarette burning out, until the long cylinder of grey ash fell from the tip and landed on my jeans.

'Christ ...'

I brushed my hand over the mess and two white streaks stretched out across my thighs. I felt a desolate emptiness setting up lodgings in the hollows of my heart; I knew the tobacco smoke wasn't going to fill it. I flicked the Marlboro onto the street and started the ignition.

It didn't seem to matter how hard I tried to rationalise what had just happened, or to push the thoughts away. Everywhere I looked was a reminder of better days, of strolls with Ben on the way to the park at Rozelle, past times when memory wasn't the predominant thought process. Was I so shallow that the dog's passing was another reminder of my own mortality; of how much of life I had squandered and how little was left to make a difference? I was dipping into melancholy and I knew it was a deep pit of despair. I flattened the pedal and beat the temporary lights outside the Tesco Express.

I took the direct route to Billy Bridge's and parked outside the hall on Cathcart Street. We'd recently seen a return of traffic wardens in the town, but the sign told me I was safe from them at this hour. The way shops were closing in the Auld Toun it seemed pointless charging for parking, but I suppose the Cooncil had to make ends meet somehow.

On the Sandgate I stopped outside the travel agents and eyed the package deals for trips to Spain.

An old giffer in a bunnet stood beside me and shook his head. 'Wouldn't fancy Turkey or Greece, this weather.'

I took his point, had seen the rioting against austerity measures on the news.

'For once Mexico seems like a safer option,' I said.

He nodded out a gruff grunt in reply and was off. I turned away myself; a holiday seemed like a waste of money in my current mindset.

In Billy's I spied Andy at the bar, half way down a pint

of heavy. He raised the glass and smiled as I approached.

'How do, mate?'

'Andy ...'

'Can I get you a pint?'

'Aye, please ...'

I pulled out a barstool, but just to rest my foot on the side of it. Since my last hospital visit my back was too delicate to sit on a hard stool for any length of time; still, I was lucky to be alive, that's what the papers said.

'So, to what do I owe the misfortune?' I said.

'Just needed a night out the house,' said Andy. 'You know how it gets to you.'

I did that. My life was a battle against boredom these days. I knew every inch of the four walls of the lounge. Early retirement had been forced upon me, it wasn't an option I'd have went for on my own steam.

'You must miss the action from your days on the force?'

My pint arrived, I sipped the head. 'Sometimes.'

'Only sometimes ... Come on, you're climbing the walls, I bet.'

There was something about Andy's expression that got me thinking, the way he seemed to be selling me on an idea all of his own.

I played along. 'It's not like the telly, y'know, it's a job like any other.'

He swayed on his stool, seemed to lilt to the side. 'Oh, go away. You wouldn't have got involved in that young girl's murder business if you didn't miss the cut and thrust!'

I felt a wry smile creep up the side of my face. I knew exactly what he was talking about, but I'd had my own reasons for getting involved in that investigation; not least the oldest excuse in the book.

I sidetracked. 'Quiet in here tonight.'

Andy's brows dropped. He was obviously happy

keeping the conversation on track. 'Look, I always wanted to ask you about that ... you made quite a name for yourself in Auld Ayr, y'know that!'

'Did I now?'

Andy put his pint down, tapped his fingers together and made dizzying revolutions with his thumbs. I could see he was concentrating; it was a new look. Mostly, Andy concentrated on where the next pint was coming from.

'Who have you been talking to, Andy?'

'*What? Me?* ... No one.'

I waited for the conspiratorial wink, it was such an obvious lie, but none came.

'Andy, you've been preparing the ground since I came in; before, even, if you include the phone call. Now either someone has put you up to this, or you're in some kind of bother yourself, credit me with some of the skills you've just been talking about.'

He sighed, let his eyes wander left to right and then he straightened his back.

'Well, let's just say, for the sake of it, that I knew someone who knew of you but didn't know how to get in touch ...'

'Okay, let's say that. Go on.'

'And, well, this someone was very interested in putting some work your way ...'

I lowered my pint, started to button my jacket. 'And there would be a drink in it for you, no doubt.'

'No way.' He leaned back, opened and closed his mouth quickly. 'Well, only a small one ...'

'Thanks, but no thanks, Andy.' I headed for the door.

'Doug ... Doug ...'

I heard Andy running behind me, as I reached the street he clutched my arm.

'Doug, please, just hear me out ... this isn't just anybody we're talking about.' He swayed in the doorway for a moment, glanced down to the street then shuffled towards me. 'Look, I was asked to give you this.'

I stopped still. 'You were what?'

Andy reached behind him and withdrew a small manila envelope from his back pocket. 'I don't know what's in it, but then, maybe that's for the best.'

Chapter 3

I headed back up the street with Andy's envelope in my hand. I didn't look at it, or even consider what accepting it might mean; merely forced it into my inside pocket and tried to forget it was there. I didn't want to become known as the Auld Toun's default gumshoe, that was never an ambition of mine, but I could tell by the desperate look in Andy's eyes that I might not be given an option on that front.

In Ayr, like every other small town, people talked. They talked about who you were and what you were. Mostly – it might have been a peculiarly west-coast thing – they liked to talk about people who were *somebody*. If you made money, you were *somebody* and if you made headlines you were *somebody*. Ayr liked to know who was walking its streets, or liked to think it did. People traded gossip about each other like football stickers, it didn't matter the accuracy, so long as it won them points on the cobbles of New Market Street or under the bus stop's shelter. It was currency and I needed to accept that my stock was up right now.

At the car I halted and turned my gaze back towards the Sandgate; I could just make out the barber's dummy in the window of Levano's. I smiled and shook my head, sometimes the familiar felt good but I knew its influence was a finite thing; I was wondering how long I would last here.

It had been a good move coming back after my divorce, and the sacking from the force. I had time to lick my wounds, recuperate even. But now I felt like a man with a neon light above his head wherever he went. Options would have to be weighed, I knew it.

My mobile let out a chirp.

It was a text:

I saw you today, but didn't know if I should speak.

'What the hell?'

There was no contact or name attached to the number, which I didn't recognise.

I felt the edges of my eyes creasing, it was a move shy of head-scratching consternation.

I stared at the screen of my iPhone, my one concession to modernity. 'Who's this?'

It didn't make any sense. I hadn't made any new contacts of late. I'd deleted a few, though – maybe it was one of them.

I put the key in the ignition and started the car. At the end of the street I looked around to see if there was anyone I recognised, but there was just a couple of snoutcasts outside Billy Bridge's and a man carrying a *Glasgow Herald* and a pint of milk from the newsagents across the road. I shook it off and headed for home.

Outside the old cattle market I dropped the gears and contemplated a trip into Morrison's to collect a ready meal for one, but the prospect seemed just too depressing. At the roundabout I upped the revs. By Belmont I heard my phone chime again.

It was another text, but I didn't pull over. The level-crossing was flashing up ahead; I followed the slowing queue of traffic and stopped just short of a Range Rover bearing the obligatory 'Ayr' number plate.

'Pretentious git,' I mumbled as I reached for the phone and went into my texts.

I didn't think you'd reply, please don't think I blame you.

I stared at the screen for a moment, tried to disinter some hint of understanding, but none came. It wasn't a tone I recognised, if you could retrieve someone's tone from a mere text.

'I don't get it.' My head shook on auto-pilot.

I heard the train coming and looked up. A passenger carriage with children pressed up to the window, waving at the row of vehicles. I stared at the bright image, sweeping past my eyes in a blur, but failed to make any sense of it.

I knew my emotions were all over the place after taking Ben to the veterinary. It wasn't so long since I'd buried my mother and very soon I'd have to box up her house and sell it on. I felt raw, too raw to use my mind for anything more than the most facile of tasks – eating, drinking sleeping, I could just about manage. But something told me the world was about to impress itself on me in its usual testing fashion.

The barrier gates started to rise and the lights flashed at the sides of the crossing. The Range Rover proceeded forward, over the Maybole Road, towards the high-walled mansions of greater Alloway; I took the left towards my mother's more modest abode.

The pizza shop was too good to pass, so I grabbed another junk-food dinner and promised to stock up on the Lean Cuisines tomorrow. It was a promise I made to myself daily, I was good at making it, bad at acting it out.

In the driveway I collected the pizza box and pointed the key ring at the car; the blinkers flashed once to tell me it was secure. As I walked into my old family home I could still smell the dog's confinement; he'd hardly ventured out of doors in weeks. The familiar smell haunted the house with all the other ghosts. Every room was a stack of memories from years gone by. My father in his retirement, snoozing in his armchair or checking the form at Chepstow. My mother,

Tony Black

in her latter years, drunken insensate, a litter of bottles at her feet as she cried for her lost days, her lost hope.

I wandered through to the kitchen and took Ben's lead from my pocket for the last time. I placed it on the worktop and it sat at first unfurling from its coil like a thin red snake, then motionless and accusatory, brazen with the weight of its inert meaning. I snatched it up and placed it in the bin.

As I turned back to the pizza box, opened up and stared at the soggy, dough-heavy article where it had slid to one side – dispensing the greater share of toppings and congealing cheese – I knew I'd lost my appetite. I turned over the lid and removed myself to the living room.

In my father's chair I reached into my coat pocket and felt for the envelope Andy had handed me outside Billy Bridge's Bar. I tapped the edge of the manila-coloured envelope against the chair's arm and sighed. There was no writing on the front, or back, nothing to help me infer its contents.

If I wanted to know what, or who, had put Andy on such a knife-edge, there was only one way I was going to find out. But I had to ask myself, first: did I really want to?

Chapter 4

The letter was in a strange hand, neat and tidy, though lacking the finer points of spelling and grammar. I could tell the words were a man's – it had been signed by a man – but the handwriting was definitely a woman's: I hadn't met a man yet that put little circles above the letter 'i'.

It could have been a joint effort – a husband and wife – but the feeling I got from the tone was more of a man dictating his thoughts. He was gruff, too. Blunt, a solid Ayrshire straight-talker. The kind I'd met a million times before, the kind that liked the sound of their own voice.

Nothing in the letter inspired me to delve further, except the mention of one name: Steven Nichols. Maybe it was the close ring of the old Liverpool super-sub that got my attention, or maybe I had seen it somewhere before. Either way I was unmoved by the prospect of delving into a cold case involving the murder of a local lad that the police had shoved in the 'too hard' drawer.

'No thanks, Andy ...'

I put the letter back in the envelope and eased further into the chair. I was sparking up a cigarette when a thought occurred to me: what was Andy thinking? In that strange way that the real world has of intruding on your thoughts, my mobile started to ring.

It was Andy. 'Hello, Doug, have you read the letter?'

I inhaled deep on my cigarette, let the smoke trail reach the ceiling before I answered. 'I have, yeah.'

'And?' His voice sounded anxious.

I tapped the edge of the letter, spoke. 'This Nichols lad ... I know the name.'

'Yeah, it was in all the papers ... you probably read about it in *The Post*, they went to town on it, him being a local lad and all that.'

It made sense. I could have stored the name away subliminally, it was certainly the kind of story that I'd follow in the paper. I took another drag on my cigarette, tried to figure a way to tell Andy this didn't seem like my kind of thing. 'Look, mate, I have to be honest ...'

He cut in. 'Yeah, the Nichols lad was one of the Order, there's no love lost between them and the police these days.'

'What Order?'

'The laddos, the Orange Men ... he was a marcher, used to run with some big names in the town and was very flash with it, by all accounts.'

If Andy was trying to make this case more appealing, inspire me to take it on, he was having the opposite effect. The loss of another flute-playing bigot in a bowler hat was not something that bothered me one iota. It was a mystery to me why, at the one point on the calendar that Ayrshire had any decent weather, we still had these people parading through the streets, booted and suited, in their little orange sashes.

'I can't say my interest is sparked by this, Andy; I'm sorry, I just don't want to get involved in that sad little world.'

'But ... they asked for you especially!' He sounded incredulous.

'Who, the Nichols'?'

'No, Davie Grant ...'

I took out the letter, checked the name. It matched. 'Should I be as impressed by the name as you sound, Andy?'

'Davie is the top man in the Order, he's a good friend of Steven's father, Bert, and he's not a happy man. Look, Davie's got deep pockets and he knows your form, Doug, I'm sure you'd be well looked after on the money side.'

'And what exactly's in this for you, Andy?'

'You know the score, finders keepers, I found you ... like you said, I get a drink for my trouble, and I really need this drink, mate.'

I was in a difficult situation; I liked Andy, he was an old face from the past and I'd always been a sucker for those connections, perhaps that's why I was still in Ayr. But I knew from my time on the force in Belfast that any crime with religious undertones could get very messy.

'Andy, you said yourself the police have laid this one to rest. What makes you think I can do any better?'

His voice rose, became lyrical. 'Well, you can try. Maybe they missed something.'

'I doubt it.'

'But you won't know until you try.'

'Andy, I've got a lot on now, I've got my mother's house to pack up and sell, and ...'

His voice sliced me like a saw-blade, 'Look, have a word, talk to the man, if you don't like what he has to say *then* think about passing it up. Will you do that for me, for an old friend?'

He knew he had me. I could hardly say no.

'Alright, but I'm promising nothing.'

'Brilliant!' His spirits audibly lifted. 'You won't regret this.'

I knew as soon as he said the word, I probably would.

I hung up the phone.

I found myself shaking my head as I tapped Steven Nichols into my iPhone and pressed search. The top hits in the Google list were from newspapers; I opted for Ayrshire's paper of note and waited for the page to load.

There was a photo: Steven looked like just another lad enjoying a pint in a rowdy pub. Those pictures tell their own story. He was holding a Rangers scarf in the other hand so was clearly celebrating an old victory, because winning the Third Division wasn't worth shouting about. The paper seemed to have given a lot of coverage to the story, the full details of his death by stabbing – just yards from his home – and the subsequent police investigation.

I recognised one of the names attached to a police quote, DI John Scott, who said they were pursuing a line of inquiry that Nichols had been the victim of a random street brawl.

'Oh, really?' I shook my head. Street brawls were impulsive acts, they took place outside pubs, clubs, taxi ranks, not in leafy residential Prestwick, a sobering half hour walk from the foot of the town.

The circumstances of Steven Nichols' death left me with more than a few questions, and none that I'd like to find the answers to. I cursed Andy again and returned to my cigarette.

Chapter 5

Something was wrong with my old home town of Ayr. It was as if invisible hands were choking the life out of it, cutting off the vital blood supply somewhere south of the High Street's middle. I stood outside Markies with an eye on the empty shops surrounding Fish Cross. Only a pound store and a charity shop kept the march of shuttered fronts at bay. I remembered a busy car accessory store had stood there, before it was whisked off to one of the out-of-town sites. That's where everything seemed to be now; somewhere else, somewhere *out-of-town*. Nobody wanted to be here now, or so it seemed. I knew the jury was out on my own intentions. I felt myself sinking deeper into a landscape that was abstract to me now. The Auld Toun I knew was gone, if it ever existed; it was a figment of my imagination, a romantic notion to file away with my store of Burns' quotes.

'Auld Ayr, wham ne'er a toon surpasses.'

Only a cynic with a nice line in sarcasm would turn that phrase now.

I smiled to myself, walked on, and wondered what Rabbie would be reeling out for the masses of today.

I knew my vision of the place was now coloured by the blunt shock of my homecoming: my mother's death, the bitter loss of a wife and profession, and the inevitable disaster of a rebounded relationship. I didn't want to think about any of that, though. I didn't want to think at all, to tell the truth, so perhaps Andy's wild goose chase was just the kind of distraction I needed.

The horn of an old VW Polo soughed a limp announcement that my friend had arrived. Andy peered over the rim of the wheel and waved a hand at me. I nodded and crossed the street towards the car; the door made the unmistakeable screech of metal on metal, like an engraver's point putting its shrill wince upon my spine.

'Andy, wherever you're taking me, I hope it's not far in this biscuit tin,' I said, tugging on the seatbelt.

'No. Not far. Davie Grant just stays in Dalmellington.'

I turned in my seat as he over-revved the engine to encourage the biting point. 'Davie Grant ... I thought you'd be taking me to see the boy's father.'

'Davie knew the Nichols lad, and he's the one picking up the tab, so ...'

I watched the lights change up ahead. 'I want to see the lad's father, not the author of that semi-literate letter.'

'Aye, and we will ... I just thought that Davie would be useful, y'know, for our investigation.'

I coughed back a guffaw. I could already see Andy sizing himself up to play Tonto to my Lone Ranger. It wasn't happening.

'Andy, couple of ground rules ... One, I do the thinking. And, two, there's no *we* here. You can limit yourself to introductions, right?'

'Okay. Okay.' He widened his eyes, glowered at me. 'Just trying to be of some help, that's all.'

I wound down my window and sparked up a cigarette; it didn't seem worth asking for permission. On the way to Dalmellington I sat back and watched the green fields stretch along the bourne of the by-pass. It was farmland, for now, but more and more suburban-style housing was creeping out this way. Will it change the place, I wondered? I knew it would, but then change was long overdue.

At the Whitletts Roundabout I watched Andy shake his head at the confusion of lanes and lights, then summon the horn again when a girl in an Aygo tried to move out. We were near Mossblown, I knew they marched there, like they did in most of these villages at the end of June. It's barbecue weather now, surely people have better things to do at this point in the development of the human race, I thought.

'I think you'll get along with Davie,' said Andy. 'He's salt of the earth.'

'I'll make my own mind up about that,' I said, knowing that I'd already let his pastime influence me some way before our introduction.

'Tell me, Andy, how do you know these people?' They didn't seem his sort, but he was fond of saying live and let live.

'Och, we go way back. Who can say, football maybe, the piping ... aye, that was probably it, I remember Davie hired me to play the pipes for one of their get-togethers.'

It was a plausible connection, Andy was one of those kent faces who found it impossible to cross the road without shaking hands with someone. I think even the strays in the street approached him for a pat on the head.

The property wasn't quite in Dalmellington, but on the long, steep incline of rough and ready road that tricked you into the village with sweeping views of the hills. There was a couple of white vans parked out front and a bulky man with a ruddy complexion stood, square footed and sure, hosing down the lawn. His rotund gut was held in check by two buttons on a short-sleeved shirt, the chest-rug above was something Connery would have been intimidated by.

'I didn't think we were going to spot the Yeti today,' I said.

Andy laughed. 'You need a second skin to survive in these badlands!'

The car slowed to a halt, grinding gravel beneath the wheels. I was still removing my seatbelt, opening the door, as Andy made a sprint for the front of the car and Davie Grant's outstretched hand. I'd never seen him play the sycophant before, this was a first for me, and I was sure I didn't like it.

I got out and greeted our host. 'Hello ...'

'So you're the boy they kicked off the force.' Davie's opener was a calculated put-down of the type I'd become depressingly familiar with, growing up on the west-coast. It was a variant form of the *get your retaliation in first* philosophy. I had thought this type of patter was dying out, but obviously not; I was never surprised to find the world was populated by more meat-heads than even I could conceive.

Something told me I wasn't going to get along with Davie Grant, as he eyed me like Cro-Magnon man peering from his cave lair.

Chapter 6

The house wasn't your typical edge of Dalmellington abode. It was bigger, for a start, the side-wings and back massively extended – but not sympathetically, it had to be said. They were boxes added to let people know they weren't part of the original home. The result was a gaudy McMansion, the kind of thing a crass new footballer's wife might go for, or a lottery winner with more luck than taste.

We walked inside; the polished-stone floors seemed newly buffed, the whole place sparkled. Davie gave the directions to follow him.

'Down the back, there, we'll sit in the conservatory, it's just through the kitchen.'

I felt like a fly in ointment walking through the hallway; the walls were covered in large, glossy photographs of Davie and a peroxide blonde half his age that I presumed to be a trophy wife. Every shot was taken under blissfully blue skies; foreign skies, not Scottish for sure. In one Davie sat on the back of a yacht, on the other he held up a large cobalt-blue fish, his bloody fingers hooked under its gills. The fish looked like a Marlin, a beautiful creature, even with its silvery underside cleaved asunder. I'd read about these fish being on the verge of the endangered list, but as Davie grinned for the camera he didn't appear to give a rat's.

Our host stopped at the kitchen island. 'The wife's pride and joy, this, you don't want to know how much it cost me ...'

He was right, I didn't. But something told me he was going to tell me anyway.

'More than my first house,' he said. 'Ten grand more than my first house, to be precise.'

I watched Andy purse his lips and start to let out a shrill whistle but I tried to look unimpressed. After all, I'd been living in my parents' home in Alloway for the last few months and grown accustomed to the bragging rights some people attach to their lifestyle. It was pathetic, to reach middle-age and think that material gain was a yardstick of worth. I'd been a police officer long enough to know that most people just used money as an excuse for bad behaviour.

'Is your wife not at home today, Davie?' My words forced a crease into his heavy brows.

'What do you want her for?' He raised his hands, showed palms.

'Just asking, that's all ... If I'd spent more than ten grand on a kitchen I'd be living in it.'

He smiled, a piranha smirk that split his broad face in two. I saw he liked my mention of his spending power; his ego was tragically transparent.

'Drinks, gents!' Davie clapped hands together and led us through to the conservatory as he prepared a jug of something bright-coloured and sweet. He was well out of earshot when I spoke again.

'Andy, what the hell have you got me into?'

'Eh?' He fiddled with a little silver ornament. 'Feel the weight of that ... bet it's solid, as well.'

I took the item from him, a little silver swan, and placed it back on the table. 'Tell me this guy is legit and I'll eat my hat.'

His eyes retreated into his head. 'Big Davie's sound as

a pound, Doug.' He painted a look of mock indignation on his face. 'Do you honestly think I would get you involved in anything shady?'

I felt myself bite on my lower lip as I turned away from him. I didn't want to answer that question.

Davie appeared in the doorway with a tray of drinks. 'Right, dive in!'

The drink was iced, but didn't cool my temper off any. I wanted to bolt, get back to my life and carry on with my normal, boring existence, but with Andy as the driver I was trapped. I felt a deep urge swell in me to plant a foot in his backside for bringing me here.

'I was saying to Doug,' said Andy, 'that the man to see about the young Nichols lad is yourself.'

Davie sat down with his thick flanks spread forward, feet up on the chair in front. 'Tragic business,' he shook his head in limp sympathy. 'Very sad business indeed.'

I wanted to ask, 'For who?' But I got the impression Davie Grant didn't like direct questions. And besides, he was fond of his own voice; I'd only be interrupting.

Davie went on: 'I knew that lad from when he was knee-high to a grasshopper. His father's a good Orangeman, as well.'

'That would be Bert?' I said.

'Bert Nichols, yes ... He's one of our own, and we look after our own.'

Andy started the nodding dog treatment. I looked away from him and fixed on Davie. 'I'm a bit confused. You see, Andy told me it was Bert Nichols who wanted to hire me to look into his son's death. If that's the case, why am I not talking to him?'

Andy started to speak but was cut down by Davie's flagging hand. 'You're correct, son, on both counts.' He put down his drink and sat forward; a tyre of gut spilled from beneath his shirt. 'We're all one big family here, you understand. When Stevie Nichols took that knife in his heart it was a wound to us all, not just his father.'

It had the ring of a cult to me. 'So you see yourself as Stevie's father, do you?'

He didn't like that, but masked the reaction with a smile. 'Like I say, we're family. And if somebody hurts my family, you can guarantee I'm going to have something to say about that.'

His tone petered into menace on the final words. It was a subtle indicator that he was not a man to be messed with, as if that was in any doubt. I knew I didn't want to be beholden to someone like Davie Grant and that's what I sensed this visit was about: *he* was hiring me to look into Stevie Nichols' death. Why he wanted to do that I didn't know, but I wasn't buying the 'we're all Orangemen together' line. If I had a vague feeling before that there was much more to Stevie's murder than a random street stabbing, then I was certain now. Call it a nose for trouble or the inalienable need of a cop to see wrongs put right, but the case had my attention now.

'Andy's told you about my fees, I take it?' I said.

Davie pressed out another sly smile, stood up with his hand out. 'You've no worries on that front, Mr Michie.'

As he gripped my hand, held tight, all I could think of was those beefy fingers of his sticking in the Marlin's bloody gills.

Chapter 7

A white Range Rover was pulling into the driveway as Davie Grant stood on his front doorstep waving to Andy and myself. I recognised the girl behind the wheel at once; and she was a girl; if you were to call her a woman you'd append the word 'barely'.

Davie called out to his young wife, 'Don't tell me the shops shut early!'

The girl drew me a sour look, turned her gaze on Andy for a minute and then stomped towards the house with the sharp points of her high heels firing like gunshots. When she reached Davie she pushed past him and he spun round before shouting out her name.

'Cassie ...' His hands were in fists, as he showed us his back he slammed the door with the heel of his hand.

'What do you think her problem is?' I asked Andy.

He was looking at the Range Rover's badge, it read *Evoque*. 'How much do you think one of these would set you back?'

I could hear voices raised in the house. 'A bundle, you can bet on that.'

Andy straightened himself and sighed as we made for his battered VW Polo.

'There's more to life than a flashy motor, mate,' I said.

He started the engine; it coughed and spluttered. 'I know, there's the likes of Cassie as well.'

I grinned to appease him but didn't think for a moment that Davie was getting the return he'd anticipated from this particular investment; Cassie looked like another source of stress for the businessman.

We took to the road, the sun starting to shine down on the roaming flats of Burns Country. The occasional bow-bent tree genuflected beyond the greens and browns and glinting coppers.

'*Auld Hermit Ayr staw thro' his woods ... An ancient borough rear'd her head ...*'

'What's that poetry?' said Andy.

'It's Burns, you heathen!'

His brows creased in a blunt plumb line. 'I'll take your word for it.'

I changed tack, got onto more familiar territory for my friend. 'It's a funny old town, Ayr, is it not?'

'You'll not get any argument from me, there.' Andy loosened his grip on the wheel, settled into his seat and kept his eyes front. 'Some of its folk are queer enough to spout poetry!'

I laughed and turned towards him; workmen in high-vis jackets had started to cone off the other side of the road, a sticky load of tar glistened from the black of a lorry, its slug line smear shining in the hot sun. 'How did Davie Grant make his money?'

Andy brightened at the change of subject. 'Well, that's a question I can answer. He had a quarry, still does as far as I know, but it's mostly played out now. He had his own trucks at the quarry, you know, for the hauling and that ... that's where he makes most his money now, at the haulage.'

I smiled. 'He makes one hand feed the other ...'

'You could say that ... But Davie Grant is a man with his

fingers in several pies. He's got a few puggies, you know, amusement arcades, as well. Oh and there's a stack of flats he rents in the town, I think they call them executive apartments.'

'So that's how he can afford to keep Cassie in her Jimmy Choos.'

'What ...?'

I shook my head. 'Never mind.'

I kept my impressions of Davie Grant, his wife, and their marital set-up in the wilds of Dalmellington to myself for the remainder of the journey back to Ayr. As we pulled off the by-pass onto the Maybole Road at the edge of Alloway, I released my seat belt and pointed out my mother's house to Andy.

He slowed the car to a halt. 'When are you putting the house on the market?'

'Soon.'

'Must be tough.'

'It's the old family home, lot of memories in there.'

Andy nodded, drummed two fingers on the rim of the steering wheel. 'Well, if you need any help, with the moving and that, let me know.'

'Going to ask Davie for one of his flats, are you?'

'That'll be right ... you couldn't afford his rents!'

As Andy pulled out I waved him off. I stood at the foot of the path, beams of sunlight lancing from the sky, as I eyed the neighbour's lawn. It was perfectly manicured, the mower must have been guided by a sextant, I thought. The lawn I was responsible for looked like an unkempt eyesore by comparison. I bowed my head and descended the path.

As I stuck the key in the door I felt a knot twisting in my gut; I was returning to an empty home, not even Ben was around anymore. The thought gored me. It was just me now; me, my demons, and a houseful of memories.

As I closed the door behind me I felt a jolt as the phone started to ring.

'Hello ...'

There was a pause on the line.

I spoke again, 'Hello ...'

A woman spoke. 'Hello, Doug.'

I recognised the voice at once, it sparked a dizzying rush inside my head. I was confused, this was the last person I had expected to hear from. When we had parted, it was final and not on exactly the best of terms.

'Lyn ... I can't believe it's you.'

A sigh; I imagined her twisting the phone cord nervously in her fingers. 'Well, I-I sent you a few texts but didn't get a reply ... I thought you must have changed your number.'

I lowered myself onto the stairs, sat. 'Ah, now that explains one mystery.'

'So you got them?'

I turned down the edges of my mouth, knew that I'd backed myself into a corner. 'I did, yeah ... to be honest, I thought someone had made a mistake.'

It was a weak excuse for my lack of reply, but she seemed to let me off the hook.

'Well, I've got you now,' she said, her tone brightening.

'Yes, Lyn, you have got me now.'

Chapter 8

I spent the night going over the case as I understood it; it seemed like a better option than going over my past history with Lyn. I'd agreed to meet her in the morning, 'just for coffee,' she'd said, but I had my reservations and never liked picking at old wounds. If Lyn had been a familiar face for me when I'd returned to the Auld Toun, she was also a nice distraction from the wreckage of my career in Ulster. I knew I'd come home to forget, to put the past behind me, and by being there Lyn seemed to do just that for me.

She represented a time in my life that I had all but closed myself off to, I'd forgotten so much of those days of our shared schooling at Ayr Academy and the sly summer pints sneaked in the beer garden of the old Bacchus. We were taking our first steps into adulthood and it was exciting, exhilarating. Neither of us was to know the years to come would be such a disappointment to us both, in our different ways.

I'd liked Lyn, when we were kids and when I'd met her again; it was an instinctual grasp for some security, not a relationship, or even a friendship, but something else entirely: familiarity. Our shared past was something solid, we could hold it in our memories, regurgitate certain moments and feel like they meant something to us. Even when all we were recounting was inanity.

'Do you remember Poolers pub?' she'd once said.

'Where was that?'

'Kyle Street, y'know round from Finnie's ...'

'Wasn't that called Legends?'

'Yeah, it was ... but that was after. Poolers had all the pool tables.'

'Oh yeah, and Legends had the pictures of Marlene Dietrich and Jimmy Dean on the walls.'

She was starting to get irritated with me; mine wasn't the memory she wanted to have, then.

'But back to Poolers ... you remember all the tables, pool tables, must have been eight or nine of them. I remember you falling for the old *what colour's that ball?* It was some hardneck, from Jabba likely, I can see him laughing at you when you said *maroon* ...'

I huffed. 'Yeah, I remember that ... didn't know whether I was going to be expected to go to the bar and buy him a drink after I'd said *it's ma-roon.*'

'It was all so new to us.'

'Yeah, it was. Back then ...'

I smiled at the thought that I was recounting the memory of us recounting a memory. It was only twelve months ago that I'd seen Lyn, said goodbye. I didn't think I'd be seeing her again so soon; I chided myself for being stupid enough to think that anything in this life was so final, surely by my age and wealth of experience I knew better than that.

I cracked the seal on another San Miguel; there was still heat in the air and the beer and weather both set me in mind of summer holidays. There was nothing in the few internet printouts that I had from the reports on the killing of Steven Nichols that spoke to me, but the visit to Davie Grant and the brush with his wife, Cassie, seemed to suggest otherwise. Call it instinct or my tried and tested assessment of the nature of people, but I knew something didn't sit right. I knew also that I didn't like the thought of messing about with a death in the Orange Order, I'd seen enough fanatics in Ulster playing the religion card.

The Nichols boy was somebody's son, though. And Andy was a friend I'd sworn to help out. The cop's call for justice still burned in me, whether the force wanted me or not.

I put down my beer and walked through to the front lounge. The place was in eerie darkness, a glabrous moon beyond the window providing just enough light for me to catch the old white net curtains billowing in the slight breeze. I reached for the light switch and flooded the scene with brightness; my eyes stung as I scanned the room for the telephone.

Bert Nichols was slow to answer; it made me wonder about the time. I checked my wristwatch, it was after eleven.

A rough throat-clearing: 'Hello ...?'

'Mr Nichols?'

'Yes. Who is this?'

I tried to ease my way into the subject subtly. 'I'm sorry to call so late, my name is Michie ... I'm an investigator, of sorts.'

'A what?'

I explained the situation, who I was. The mention of Andy and Davie Grant seemed to set some distant bells chiming in the recesses of his tired mind.

'Ah, I see. Pleased to make your acquaintance, Mr Michie.'

'I was actually hoping to meet with you, if that was at all possible?'

'At this hour?'

'I was thinking more like tomorrow afternoon.'

His voice stuttered, 'I'm afraid that won't be possible ... we are marching then, you realise.'

I'd forgotten it was the season. 'Ah ... then what about before, or after?'

'Mr Michie, I'm tied up for the entire day. I could snatch a few minutes here and there with you, but that's the best I could do – I wouldn't want you wasting a day running after me.'

'No, that's fine. I can join you before the march and take it from there.'

'Well, if you're sure.'

'Yes, I'm sure. There are a few things I need to know before I start digging.' I winced on the final, inappropriate word.

'Well, I'll see you bright and early tomorrow, Mr Michie.'

'Tomorrow it is. Goodbye.'

As I put down the phone I knew I was going to have to pick it up again right away. The fragile arrangement I'd made to meet Lyn for coffee would have to be cancelled now.

I let out a long exhalation of breath and reached for the receiver.

Chapter 9

The radio alarm woke me with the news from Razorlite that there was trouble in America.

When is there never? I thought.

I reached for the off button; I had troubles enough of my own to think about.

I dressed quickly, in the still-belted jeans by my bed, a fresh white T-shirt and a sweat-top-cum-hoodie that had seen better days. I had a fair idea there'd be people groomed to the nines where I was going – bowler hats and the lot – and I definitely didn't want to be confused with one of their number.

Bert Nichols had sounded like a square peg on the phone, but I knew that was often the case; I could recall being warned early on that it was the 'quiet ones you need to watch out for'. He was in the Orange Order, after all; that in itself took some out-there views in my book, even if he did hide his light under a bushel. Still, I was taking nothing for granted; I'd seen the loss of a child do strange things to people, some wailed like keening mothers of old and some held it in, let it fester.

The postie had come early, the mat on the hall smothered in a rainforest of glossy flyers, the top one for the Iceland store up the road. I sifted through the pile and picked out the one genuine item of mail. It was a white envelope, felt like a card; as I ripped into it my suspicions were confirmed. It was a sympathy card from the vets offering condolences on the loss of my 'good friend, Ben'. I felt a jab at my heart but it passed quickly as reality flooded back: I tipped up the card to find the bill – it wasn't there. I felt genuinely moved by the gesture, and more than a little guilty I'd been cynical enough to question their motives; I suppose, if you look hard enough, there is still some heart in this world.

I knew my way around my mother's kitchen so well by now that I could just about make my morning coffee blindfolded. 'Jesus, Doug ... don't get settled, now.'

I brushed the stubble on my chin and leaned over the sink to look out the window; flat white clouds hung in the sky, a hint of low sun burnishing their edges.

'Time to move on ...'

I knew now it was time to leave Auld Ayr. I was slowly coming to question that it had been a good move coming back at all. I couldn't figure it out, why had I returned? When I'd been shown the door by the RUC they'd made it clear Belfast was no place for me: was it fear or familiarity that drove me here? I didn't know the answer to that, but I did feel called. Perhaps that was it, to lay old ghosts to rest and move on, rebuild somewhere else. The passing thought found a new significance in my mind: I'd had to cancel on Lyn; perhaps it was for the best. She hadn't taken it well and had gone all quiet on me; she deserved a fuller explanation.

I picked up the phone and let my thumb hover over her name in the contacts book, but couldn't press it. It was something about the disappointment I knew was going to be heard in her voice. Lyn had faced enough disappointment in her life and I didn't want to be the one to shovel more on there and watch.

'Suck it up, Doug ...'

I resolved to text, a cop out I know, but that was the level I'd reached now. I had so much to face – the case, the house sale, my future – that I would be making a few more stark choices if I was to reach the end of the list in one piece.

I tipped the remainder of my coffee in the sink and snatched up my car keys. The road out to Mossblown was quiet, unusual for the A77 these days, but I wasn't knocking it.

I'd found directions for the route of the march easily enough; I figured on parking up at one of the town's two pubs and taking it from there. Mossblown was Apache country to me; it had been a mining village once, filled with decent enough types but – like everywhere else on the west-coast – now was fading fast. I pulled up at the Fourways Pub and made my way in, tried to blend. There was a group of lads pinting it already.

'See wee Arthur had his shed burnt out,' said one, an elbow on the bar but an eye on some banter.

'His shed?'

'Aye ... they think it was that flag of his they were after.'

Something seemed to be missing, it was the omnipresent smokers' pall – pubs like this seemed undressed without it, the yellowed walls were almost embarrassed on full display.

The barman came over and nodded; he took my order and joined the chatter. 'Arthur's only got himself to blame ... can't be flying a Union Jack in these times.'

I looked down the bar, the crowd were nodding. 'He kept it for the football, though.'

'Well, it might be the right colours for the 'Gers but not for the country, some would say.'

The youth raised himself off the bar and pointed a finger at the barman. 'You trying to say something?'

'All I'm saying is, there's a reason for that sign above the door!'

My pint was placed before me, some golden liquid evacuated over the edge and ran towards the beer mat. I paid up and glanced towards the door and the sign which read: NO FOOTBALL COLOURS.

The youths seemed to retreat, silenced but not calmed. I watched as one thinned eyes towards me as if trying to ascertain which foot I kicked with. I put out an unthreatening smile and headed for the window seat to hide behind my pint and the morning paper. I'd almost forgotten how tribal this part of Scotland became when football and religion entered the conversation. The running conflict was almost hard-wired in some parts of the populace. I felt my adrenaline spike as an atavistic fear rose in my chest, a programmed response that had not been called upon for decades.

I had the pint to my lips as the rowdier of the group appeared before me, tipping his head threateningly and slapping his palms on the table.

'You got some kind of problem, pal?' he said.

Chapter 10

I had problems coming out of my ears, but something told me the pencil-neck in front of me wasn't going to be adding to them, no matter how much he'd like to. There was a stock Ayrshire put-down queuing on my lips: 'I've forgotten more than you've learned, son.'

'What?'

I sat back in my seat and spread my arms behind me in the most unthreatening gesture I could manage. The yob jutted his jaw in reply, he was the sort that collected trouble around the country villages like others collected muck on their boots. I knew the type and knew the routine for dealing with them. I felt myself sighing inwardly.

'If you're thinking of noising me up, pal, you might as well pick the window you'd like to leave through now ...'

He thinned his eyes, heavy brows drooped. I'd seen the look a million times before; in uniform it had been the cause to take a step back, but I hadn't been in uniform for years – now I knew the look as the match to the blue touch-paper. I'd given him two choices: laugh it off and move away, or call in the Mossblown massive for back-up. I sat back and watched as the gerbils working the wheel inside his head put in a panic sprint.

'*What*?' The word seemed to drop out of his mouth like

drool. I wasn't playing by the rules and all pubs have rules – it was like playing pool in a pub for the first time and having to make clear two shots carry after a foul – I was merely pointing out that the local Young Team didn't play in my league.

I stood up, if there was one thing known to unsettle a prospective attacker it was the ear to ear grin: I smiled my widest, right in his face. I imagined myself knocking him over with Ultrabrite rays, but truth told, I wouldn't have needed any help. As he staggered backwards the only thought on his mind was 'get me away from this nut-job'.

When the youth retreated my view to the bar opened up; a middle-aged man in a black suit and tie was standing there with his hands clasped behind his back. When he saw me looking he took two steps forward and spoke. 'Mr Michie?'

I turned off the full-beam. 'Yes.'

He brought his hands front, allowed one to clasp the black bowler and extended the other. 'I'm Bert Nichols.'

I took his hand. 'Pleased to meet you.'

Mr Nichols refused the offer of a drink and joined me at my table. I felt a slight embarrassment for him having witnessed the fun and games with the village idiot, but after a few moments in his company it was clear to me that Bert was a wise enough man to be unperturbed by such trivia. He seemed to take his position seriously; this was a man who had just lost a son, to be suited and booted for a march so soon showed a level of dedication I hadn't counted on. Was he a zealot? My automatic assumption to all those with religion and politics was a definite yes, but there was more to him than that.

'How long have you been a marcher?' I said.

'Man and boy.' His answer was succinct, didn't require clarification.

'And I believe your son, Steven, was too ...'

His gaze met the middle distance, seemed to alter his focus. 'Yes. That he was.'

It might not have been the most subtle introduction to the subject, but having stumbled upon it now, it would be churlish not to make the most of it. I avoided a recounting of the murder and its details and tried to establish what background I could.

'Stevie was an avid supporter of your ... interest?'

He turned to face me, seemed ruffled. 'That's an unusual way of putting it.'

'How would you like me to put it?'

'Do I sense a distaste for our *interest*, Mr Michie?'

How did I answer that? I could spell it out flatly, or I could give details about how I'd grown up in the west-coast and seen school-mates' family homes with pictures of King Billy on the wall. The Battle of the Boyne was 1690, that some people were still so obsessed with it was beyond me.

I went for avoidance; it didn't serve me to put all my cards on the table right away. 'My opinions aren't relevant here. However, the fact that you ask the question makes me think both you and your son were no strangers to hostile company.'

A thin smile pressed itself on his dry lips. 'You seem an astute man, Mr Michie. I'm sure there is no question of your professionalism being compromised.'

'None whatsoever.'

He didn't reply, just looked at his watch then averted his gaze towards the window. A crowd was gathering outside.

'I'll have to be making tracks soon.'

'Of course ... before you go, can you help me out with some contacts of your son's?'

'Friends, associates, that sort of thing?'

I nodded. 'Was there a partner, a girl?'

Mr Nichols coughed into his hand. 'Yes, perhaps, at least I believe so.'

'Well, I'd like to speak to her, and any others you think may be relevant. Especially those who were with him on the night of the ...' I clamped my mouth tight.

'The murder, Mr Michie.'

'Yes.'

'I'll draw up a list and send it to you, will there be anything else?'

'Not right away. Not until I get more of a handle on the case.'

He stood up, collected his bowler and headed for the door. As he went he put a thinned stare on the group of youths I'd encountered earlier; they dropped heads towards their pints.

'They tell me you were police once.'

'That's right.'

'In Ulster, I believe.'

'You've done your own investigation.'

He raised his hat. 'Due diligence, you might call it.' He patted down the top of the bowler. 'You'll know John Scott, the investigating officer, I presume?'

His casual use of the DI's name caught me off guard. 'I know him a little ...'

'Perhaps you should get to know him a little more, Mr Michie.' He touched the rim of his hat as he left through the door.

Chapter 11

It could have been the passing of my mid-life crisis or it could have been the desire to move on, but the sporty Audi's appeal was now wearing thin. I took my thoughts back to the day I'd bought the car, fresh from Ulster and looking for a familiar place to lick my wounds; it was only a year or so ago but it seemed like forever. So much had happened, I could tot up the events in order of impact: the death of my mother, the death of the family dog, the death of my marriage, my career and the very early death of any relationship I'd had with Lyn. I knew there was one more death I could have, perhaps even should have, added to that list: my own. The person I had to thank for that not being the case was an old friend from my days on the force, Mason. He wouldn't hear tell of thanks though; truth told, he wanted as little to do with me as possible.

I pulled over at the Tesco Express on the Maybole Road, I still had the car park fixed as the old Anfield Hotel in my mind, couldn't quite come to terms with another self-service outlet adding to the sprawling Tesco empire. When I was a kid, you'd be embarrassed beyond the life of you to be seen with a blue and white Tesco bag; heaven forefend you would be forced to wear Tesco trainers, if you'd suggested then the shop would take over the country, there'd have been gut-laughs all round.

I stilled the engine and took out my mobile phone. Mason's number was still on speed-dial from the last case he'd assisted me with, but hadn't been used for some time.

Ringing.

'Hello ...'

It was a gruff reply, he'd have me on caller ID so I shouldn't have been surprised.

'Is that the best you can manage?'

A tut.

'Is there a purpose to this call, Doug?'

Straight for the jugular, as ever.

I toned down my enthusiasm to re-establish the friendship. 'You know, I think it's the native Americans who have the philosophy that when you save someone's life, you become responsible for them.'

'I'm a native of Cumnock.'

'I've heard the town called Dodge City. Isn't that the wild west?'

He huffed down the line. 'I think it's more to do with the number of benefits claimants.'

The way this Tory government were going I could see the town becoming a tent city soon. 'If *call me Dave* gets his way they might have to break out the bivouac ... have you still got your tepee?'

He shuffled the phone to his other hand, I heard an office door creak. 'Right. Enough banter, is there something you want?'

'I'm on my way out to the Maclaurin Galleries ...'

'Rozelle?'

The last time we worked together we'd met in the similarly private setting of Belleisle; I presumed the locality would spark his interest, or at least make him a little curious.

'I've not been out that way for a while. Maybe I'll join you.'

'I'm on my way now.'

He clicked off.

I'd grown up around this way, all the streets were depressingly familiar and haunted by ghosts of childhood memories. Times plunking school, fagging it on ten Regal bought with the money in my father's coin bottle. Football matches against the Belmont Academy team, their coach with the hair sprayed into a crash helmet, who would never head the ball. On my way back to the Auld Toun, these reminiscences had been a comfort, a familiar old coat I threw on and pretended to be the younger man I once was. Now they were just distractions, odd jarring flashbacks that served only to make me feel like an anachronism. I was out of place, out of time; I needed to move on and I needed Mason to help me with that.

As I pulled into the car park a dog walker jerked the lead tight and scolded an energetic spaniel. The sight burned me, reminded me when Ben was like that. I stilled the engine and raised eyes to the sky.

'Get a grip, Michie,' I told myself. My mind was wandering and that was no state to be in on a murder investigation; when you get sloppy, things go wrong.

I locked the car and headed through to the gallery. There was a permanent exhibition, the late Alexander Goudie's paintings of the epic Tam O'Shanter poem. I didn't need an excuse to come and wallow in Burns' genius, but every time I did I was transported to the work, the dark night when '... *chapman billies leave the street, And drouthy neibors, neibors, meet ...*'

I was admiring Goudie's work, his fine detailing of the infamous grey mare, Meg, when I became dimly aware of another presence in the room.

'A better never lifted leg ...'

As I turned around I spied Mason, he put his hand out.

'Hello, Doug.'

'How's things?' I said.

'In general or in the force?'

I tilted my head, 'Are you still allowed to call it that, thought you were the Police Service now?'

'Aye well, don't get me started.'

The ice-breaking had went better than I hoped, as we padded about the gallery we shared conversation in hushed tones, right up until '*Kirk-Alloway was drawing nigh*' and Mason lost his patience with all the small chat.

'So, what's this about, Doug?'

'*This*?'

He raised a hand, placed the flat of his palm on my chest. 'Don't even attempt to disguise the fact you have another agenda.'

'That sounds even worse than an ulterior motive.'

He removed the hand and covered his eyes in disbelief.

'Look ... I'm leaving town.'

He seemed unfazed. 'I don't remember a big goodbye when you went to Ulster.'

I let out a defeated sigh; it was histrionics and Mason knew it but the elaborate *pas de deux* felt like custom now. 'Okay, and I'm on a case.'

'What in the ... do you forget how the last one ended?'

'Mason. This isn't like that, I'm doing a favour ...'

'Yeah, let me guess, for a friend.'

'That's right, but I assure you this is my last hurrah and then I'm moving on, I've had it with Ayr.'

Now he smiled. 'And, boy, Doug Michie, has Ayr had it with you.'

'What are you on about?'

The smile subsided as he started to fasten the buttons of his coat. 'Sorry, I believe that was a straw man projection ... what I meant to say is, I've had it with you, Doug. So, don't think of asking me to sneak out case files or snoop on fellow officers, or what's that other favourite of yours? Oh yeah, save your sorry backside from oblivion!'

Mason's strides to the door were heavy with the satisfaction of a man who had spoken his mind. He got as far as the doorway before I called out to him.

'It suits you, Mason ... the *Detective Inspector* title, that is.'

He stopped dead in his tracks, spun. 'What's that supposed to mean?'

I walked slowly towards him, dropped my voice to a less confrontational volume and said: 'It means, you did alright out of your last involvement with one of my cases.'

My last point hung in the air between us like a noxious gas that threatened dire consequences.

Chapter 12

Mason waited until I drew level with him and then he uttered one word: 'Outside.'

I trailed him down the heavy stone steps, we remained unspeaking but the sound of shoe leather on bare stone resounded with us. I thought about a placatory comment, something to claw back the barbs in the last one, but nothing came to me. I'd known Mason for so long that he would likely see through it anyway, brush it aside with a put-down riding point.

Mason was first through the front door, pushing so hard the hinges screamed out. In the street he pointed me to the car park and started to move in long, loping strides.

'Look this is ridiculous,' I called out.

He turned and put the serious eye on me. 'We'll talk in the car.'

I held up my palms and followed behind him once again; what was the point in arguing? He was either going to help out or not, even the old pals act wore thin eventually.

Mason had parked next to me, a silver BMW. I watched the blinkers flash as he opened up, and clocked the badge on the rear.

'Man, they sprung for the five series ...' the words were out before I realised their import.

'I'm warning you, Doug, don't start trying to cash-in favours.' He had the cheek to point his finger at me, as if to ram home the message. 'Now get in.'

I closed the door gently, ran a reassuring hand over the leather dash. I knew I was making a 'big spender' face when he turned to front me and spoke again, through his lower teeth this time.

'If one of us owes the other something, then I'm the one that should be collecting, Doug.'

'Look, I don't want to argue the toss with you ...'

He cut in. 'Because you know I'm right. What am I?'

'I nodded. Yes, Mason, you're right.'

'Grand, then we're sorted.' He removed the car key from his pocket and put it in the ignition. He glanced my way again. 'Are you still here?'

'Now that you're a DI, and moving in some rarefied circles no doubt, what's your impression been of John Scott?'

Mason pushed himself further back in the driver's seat, it was as if he was trying to ease himself out of discomfort. 'John's one of the boys, you know that.'

'He's Craft, you mean?'

'Along with a fair portion of the others in King Street. I've no reason to believe it compromises him, he's a top operator as far as I know.'

I thought his answer was a little too diplomatic, like his new rank had altered his thinking.

'That was a very quick response.'

'I'm a quick lad ... now what's this about?'

I told him what I knew about the street stabbing of Stevie Nichols. About his connections to the Orange boys, about his father's standing in the Order and about my invitation from Davie Grant to look into the case further. All the while Mason sat silently, taking it all in. If there was an ounce of interest flickering in those eyes of his, I missed it.

He stalled before responding, drummed his fingers on the steering wheel. 'Now, if I didn't know John Scott was the investigating officer on that case, this would be my chance to ask why you dropped his name ...'

I shook my head. 'If only it was so simple; the victim's father suggested Scott might be a good first step on my investigation.'

Mason gripped the wheel, looked front. 'Now, why would he do that?'

'That's what I wondered, and then you confirmed for me that he's a player in the Craft.'

'Now wait a minute, that lot have had their fingers well and truly burnt lately. I don't see there being any connection there at all.'

The windows in the car were starting to steam up and I could feel my lungs calling out for nicotine. I eased the door open and motioned Mason outside. As I lit us up I sensed a marked change in his demeanour.

'Well, now I have your interest let me run a theory by you ...'

He inhaled deep. 'Go on.'

'Let's suppose we don't buy the verdict of a street stabbing by some un-named rowdy.'

'Oh, Doug, come on ... you're dumping your rubbish on my doorstep again.'

I flagged him down, held my cigarette like a dart to emphasise my points. 'Well, it was in leafy Prestwick, and just about on the lad's doorstep, so not exactly by the book. But, that aside, why is the Order's top boy hiring me to go over it again when he knows the very friendly DI Scott will surely have done a thorough job?'

Mason eased his elbow onto the roof of the BMW and looked out to the copse of trees on the edge of the car park.

'You have me there, it doesn't make any sense ... unless there's some kind of internal wrangle.'

I laughed at his use of management speak. 'Is that what you'd call it these days? What about a split, a turf war, a schism ...?'

He eased his glare back to me. 'We're getting way ahead of ourselves.'

I nodded; my cig had burned down to the filter, I dowped it on the tarmac. 'Of course we are. We'd be complete and utter idiots to even suggest the like ... unless we had something to go on.'

Mason was shaking his head, easing himself back into the car. 'Don't even think about asking me to go over John Scott's work, I've got no grounds for that.'

As he closed the door the car's engine ignited, the window was starting to roll down when he turned back to me. He may have had more to say but I got my words out first. 'Electric windows, too, eh? Man, they spared no expense on this motor!'

Chapter 13

I waded my way through a gang of deadbeats in baseball caps that had set up camp at the foot of Asda bridge, thinking it was a bit of an early morning start for them. Two were arguing over a joint the size of a rolled-up bus ticket, collecting applause from the rest of the group who staggered into each other in dazed attempts to extricate the communal bottle of White Lightning. There was a time when people came here to feed the swans with their children – an old woman, Sylvia, I think her name was, used to stand sentry with a plain loaf in her hand. I wondered where she was now, where that Auld Ayr was. We seemed to have restocked the town with a new underclass of junkies and alcoholics, all content to while away their time on the streets collecting half Chelsea smiles and cabbage ears in the casual conflict that followed them like the sickly scent of their fortified wines.

'Unbelievable,' I muttered and shook my head as I made for the town centre. A chorus of onlookers seemed to reciprocate in mute sympathy.

One stepped up, announced: 'What Ayr needs is a bad batch of smack!' His face was scarlet, the sight of rowdy wasters in the street an offence to every one of his sixty-plus years. 'Aye, bad dose of smack to put the lot of them in the ground!'

It seemed a bit harsh to me, but the old fella grabbed some appreciative looks and even some soft applause from the concourse. I felt a smile creep up my face; one thing we weren't short of on the west-coast was passion.

By Fish Cross I thought I'd entered the set of some dystopian disaster movie. Both sides of the street, all the way to the Sandgate, looked shuttered up. Only the butcher seemed to be holding his own, his apron-clad manikin putting on a defiantly jolly expression in the face of the grim apocalypse that had gripped the town. The answer seemed to be to copy everyone else and walk with my head down towards the shifting centre of our dwindling commerce.

I picked out a café in the Lorne Arcade, we'd met there once before and I knew Lyn liked the coffee. It seemed strange to me that whilst half the town had slid into despair the other half had become coffee snobs with Doonfoot tractors and private Ayr plates.

Lyn looked up as I entered the shop, she managed a low-voltage smile that I felt compelled to acknowledge with an even dimmer one myself. Still, I felt glad to see her so cheery after I'd cancelled on her the day before.

'Hello, Lyn.'

'Thanks for coming.'

'Well, I nearly didn't.' I pulled out a chair and sat down.

'Oh ...'

I realised at once how my last statement had been taken the wrong way. 'What I mean is, I'm very busy at the moment.'

'I'd heard you'd made a bit of a name for yourself since ...' She briskly changed subject. 'Are you working a case?'

Lyn had been the last person to hire me – I might not have been the most professional investigator in the world but it didn't seem right to discuss my work with an ex-client. And that was how I wanted to see Lyn now.

I tried moving the conversation along. 'There was a bit of a hooley in progress outside the old Asda.'

Eyes rolled, a tut. 'When is there never in this town?'

'I don't suppose they confine their activities to a Saturday night in the Magic Circle anymore ...'

'No, they do not. Every day is out-your-face day when you're on a methadone programme. You see them sitting on the bench outside Boots like they're waiting for someone to hand them a menu!'

I'd seen this myself, it was almost comical how commonplace it had become. The town was awash with drugs, legal and illegal. 'Shall I order our own low-grade high?'

She smiled. 'A latte for me, please.'

The atmosphere in the coffee house was surprisingly easy-going; I'd expected an inquisition, perhaps some kind of judgement passed on my way of life, but I was soon reminded that wasn't Lyn. She was a good sort and we went too far back for any water that had passed under the bridge recently to splash us now. She spoke about her son, Glenn, and his new life at college in Edinburgh. She had a stint living with her sister on Arran and a job in the Co-op there, but she felt too isolated. She didn't sound drawn back to Ayr so much as the island bored her.

'And what about you, Doug?'

How did I answer that? 'You know, I'm getting by.'

'It must be hard for you in that big old house of your mother's. I mean, it was the family home, there must be the memories to contend with.'

She knew I had a sentimental side, that I could brood on the past. 'None of that's healthy, I know ... it's why I'm selling up.'

Her pallor lightened, eyes widened. 'Selling up?'

'It's time for a change.'

'But where will you live?' Her voice was high, plaintive.

'I hadn't thought about that.'

'Will you stay in Ayr?'

That I had an answer for. 'Oh, God, no. I'm pretty certain the Auld Toun and me have both seen better days ... it's time to go our own ways.'

Lyn put down her coffee and stared through me, she seemed to be processing my words. 'I just thought ...'

'What? That I was back for good? Never happen. It feels like a mistake just sitting here in this coffee shop talking to you – I should have left my past where it was.'

Lyn turned her face away. For a second I thought I sensed a tremble on her lips but no words came. She collected her bag from the floor and pushed out her chair. Her wide eyes seemed clogged with red vessels as she took me in.

'Lyn ...'

'I have to go.' Her voice was trembling now. 'I shouldn't have contacted you, Doug. I'm very sorry.'

Her movements were hurried as she made for the door. I thought she might turn and wave, make her sudden exit official, but she took the street at a clip and was soon out of view. I stared down at her coffee, it was still swirling in the cup. She hadn't touched a drop.

Chapter 14

I couldn't let a good cup of coffee go to waste, and it was very good coffee. Lyn's actions had shocked me a little, I knew she had been doing it hard these last few years but couldn't see the next few offering any let up. She'd went from having the weight of the world on her shoulders – all the worry a mother has about her son, and then some – to packing him off to college on the other side of the country. She was sensing the gap in her life now and with no job to occupy her she had too much time to think. If there was one thing I did know, it was that worry like that only led to more worry.

I checked my iPhone, tried to compose a placatory text, something close to a sorry, without actually using the word. I mean, I still didn't know what I was to apologise for. I felt an even keener need to get out of town quickly now – because I could see Lyn's problems becoming mine if I didn't.

As I keyed in the text, another one came through. It was from Andy.

How's things going there, Sherlock?

There was more to come, the three dots at the bottom indicating he was still typing.

Bert Nichols has given me a list of contacts, says you'll need it.

I felt my eyes start to roll upwards; Andy still seemed a little too keen to make himself an invaluable part of this investigation. For me that meant carrying dead weight at the very best, at the worst he could get himself into some bother. Until I knew exactly what we were dealing with here, Andy was going to have to be put in his place.

I texted back:

Meet me in Billy Bridge's in an hour.

I shoved the phone in my pocket, caught the ping of a reply, but was too busy grinding my teeth to read it. I paid the waiter for our coffees and turned back into the street, I had such a head of steam on me that I nearly knocked over a *Big Issue* seller at the foot of the arcade. He gave me a mouthful of what sounded like Turkish.

'Sorry, no offence, mate.'

Dark eyes burned curses at me, as he tried to gather up his dropped magazines. I bought one to placate him, handed over a couple of quid, 'Look keep the change, eh.'

A woman in a pink velour tracksuit had stopped to stare, a hand went on her hip as she scratched a white stiletto along the paving flags to trap a stray magazine. I felt like the star of my own Mr Bean movie as I made for New Market Street, away from the mêlée that was the High Street.

I sparked up a Marlboro as I went, trying to get my thoughts in order. I knew I needed to start making concrete plans towards moving on. As if pulled by invisible wires I found myself at the estate agent's window, scanning the property prices. The sums were eye-watering; even with the recent property market crash I wondered just who in this town had the cash to buy a house.

I crushed the cig under my shoe and went in.

The place was plush, clearly newly fitted out. I eyed the Eames chairs that had been pushed out front with caution, they sat side by side with a coffee machine in front of them.

I was old school, and know you don't get owt for nowt; the tray of Kit Kats was coming out my fees.

'Can I help you, sir?' She was St Tropez tanned with teeth white-towards-dazzling. It was the same look as Cassie Grant had went for – Big Brother contestant in waiting.

'I'm here to sell my house.' I knew it was still my mother's house in all but name, though there seemed no point explaining. I wanted it off my hands because it had come to feel like a weight I could do without.

'Okey-doke ... we'll need to book in a valuation first of all.'

I nodded, as she turned towards the desk she'd sprung from like a trapdoor spider. There was a brisk offer of coffee but I declined, my tastes had already shifted towards something stronger. This was a big step, final you could say. It marked the close of a particularly painful chapter in my life.

'Can you tell me how quick they're selling right now?'

'Well, it depends ... we've had some sell in a matter of months, others have been a lot slower. It's still a very difficult market.'

I thought of the wall-to-wall property porn that was on the television and the eye watering amounts of tax payer's cash that had been transferred to banks 'too big to fail' and wondered just what the attraction with home ownership was. It felt anathema to me – I wanted to be free of ties.

She took my address and telephone number, promised a prompt visit and valuation. I thanked her, added: 'The quicker the better.'

'In a hurry are you?'

'You bet.'

In the Bridge's bar Andy was stationed in his usual spot, a pint of mild in front of him that didn't seem to have been touched. An old soak was regaling him with a war story that

I knew he'd heard a hundred times at least. In kindness, or simply because he had nowhere else to go, Andy nodded sagely and pretended to be fascinated.

'A pint, please.' I turned to Andy and his companion, 'Can I get you anything?'

They both shook heads; my face seemed to be enough to break up their reverie. The old boy slunk off, a backwards glance caught me like a left hook.

'Jeez, who stole your toffee?' said Andy.

'What?'

'You have a face on you like a burst couch.'

'Thank you.' My pint came and I blew the head down the side of the glass, gulped deep. It was on my mind to tell him about Lyn, about the family home I'd just put on the market and how a knock-down price would upset my sister, but I did that guy thing of opting for a different subject altogether.

'Right, where's this list, Andy mate?'

He fished in his inside pocket and produced another sealed manila envelope. 'Here you go ... but finish your pint before you open it.'

'*What*? ... I mean, why?'

'Just, y'know, enjoy your pint first, the names aren't going to change.'

I weighed the envelope in my hand, it was a fair bundle of pages but then I'd expected a man like Bert Nichols to be thorough.

'You make it sound like there's names in here I don't want to see ...'

Andy looked away, picked up his pint and quaffed a good pelt in one clean hit.

Chapter 15

I manoeuvred Andy to the back of the pub, to the quietest spot I could find among the old tables that were scratched and scarred by heavy use. This was a serious drinkers' den, about as far removed from a style bar as you could get, and it suited me fine. There were some parts of Auld Ayr that were resistant to the march of time, to tarting up and the crass push to get in a younger, trendier crowd. A glossy cocktails menu would look as out of place here as those pictures of a Sphinx on the Moon.

It was an open area, but narrow. The walls seemed to be used to keeping secrets, which came as a comfort. Andy looked up and down the length of the bar. I put a disapproving gaze on him, felt tempted to ask what he was playing at, but let it go, for now.

'So, tell me, Andy, how did you happen to come by this list?' I removed the envelope he'd handed me earlier.

'Bert gave it to me ... he said you'd asked him for it.'

'*I* did.' My intonation didn't seem to register with Andy. I turned away and started to rip into the envelope.

It was the same handwriting I'd seen on the earlier letter Andy had delivered, the meandering semi-literate tone was a man's but the writing part a woman's. If the first letter had come from Davie Grant, I'd guess the one taking the dictation was the less than intellectually agile Cassie.

Tony Black

'What is it?' said Andy.

'You mean you actually *don't* know ...?'

He bridled. 'Of course I don't ... what are you trying to say?'

Perhaps I was just being a little paranoid, I'd known Andy longer than most, after all – if he was colluding with the Order boys to confuse me I'd know for sure, without any guesswork.

'Who wrote this note?' I said.

He shrugged, brushed a hand down the front of his jeans as he went to collect up his pint. 'I've no idea, is there some kind of a problem?'

My problem, if indeed there was one, was that Andy seemed to be acting as a go-between. He was delivering letters supposedly from Bert Nichols that might just turn out to be from Davie Grant. It could be nothing – they were all looking for the same answer, after all – but something about the set-up caused a knot to form in my stomach.

'Tell me, Andy, doesn't it strike you as strange the way Davie Grant's taking care of business?'

'What do you mean?' He supped his pint, returned it to a table-top carved in initials.

'I mean, it's Bert's son that was supposedly murdered, yet Davie Grant seems to be calling all the shots here.'

'Well, he is picking up the bill.'

There was that, and he was the type of man who could easily be described as a control freak when it came to parting with brass, but Bert Nichols was no slouch either. 'Doesn't he trust Bert?'

Andy still looked nonplussed, creasing his nose as if a repellent odour had hit him. 'Look, you're asking the wrong man. I'm just the messenger, Doug.'

I smacked the table, 'And that's another thing, I'm not happy with all communication being filtered through you ...

60

it's either my case, or it isn't.'

'Doug, they're a funny lot, you know that.'

'I'm not on about them dressing up in bowler hats and silly wee bibs ... what have they really got to hide?'

Andy leaned forward, scratched at the stubble on his chin with his thumb and forefinger then let out a long-stilled breath. 'Okay. Perhaps they're a wee bit over cautious, but wouldn't you be in their shoes? They attract haters, y'know.'

If they attracted haters it was a case of getting back what you dished out. I remembered the daft kids in the pub in Mossblown, all fired up on a bigotry they'd been spoon-fed since they could first walk. It was a west-coast of Scotland tradition that had outlived its time and was relying on recruits from the unevolved.

'That march I went to have a look at was just full of neds in 'Gers tops chucking back the bevvy. A few of the older ones had got dressed up, splashed the Old Spice, dragged the missus along at their elbow ... the women were all drinking mixers with Irn-Bru, it was sad.'

Andy got the picture. 'Och that's just spectators. There's a hard-core too.'

'What's the hard-core? Those that know the history, those that think their religion puts them a notch above the minority?'

Andy showed palms, slunk back in his chair. 'Hang on, I'm not defending them. I think it's all nonsense too, but some of them are our neighbours, some of them pay my wages now and again.'

'You're fond of preaching, aren't you, Andy?'

'Aye, I suppose so.'

I shook my head, the irony was lost on him.

As I picked up the list again and scanned the first few names I felt myself sinking deeper into a case that left a bad taste in my mouth.

'I don't like any of this, mate.'

Andy looked away, mumbled: 'You don't have to, you're getting paid.'

'I feel like I'm working for the Klan.'

'That's a bit harsh, no one's been tarred and feathered.'

'No ... only murdered.' I picked up the list and left Andy alone with his pint and his conscience.

Chapter 16

It was one of those rare days in the Auld Toun, sun splitting the clouds and people with smiles on their faces. On the way from the car park at the old cattle market I'd already spotted two teenage moshas belying their stereotype and belting out Bon Jovi. They had good crowds, but couldn't compete with the Mexican salsa band that had set up outside Wallace Tower. This lot had an amp, it created a fair racket but the crowd seemed to love it. Even the boys on the fruit and veg stall were tapping their feet in between bouts of patter with their punters.

I looked for a gap in the stream of busses and blue-badge holders and made my way towards the bookshop. The window seemed to be short on a vital ingredient: books. There was a stack of toys and games, I could see a table of Kindles beyond the door, but the books were in short supply. The two they did have featured the smug coupons of Jamie Oliver and Duncan Bannatyne beaming back at me. I was never less tempted to enter a shop. I felt a sinking feeling inside me and longed for the days of the old James Thin store on the Sandgate.

I was sparking up a red-top when I spotted a figure waving at me from across the road. She was at the top of Nile Court, under the great arch, and shimmying round a nascent queue at the ATM. I freed myself from a slouch to return the wave, then waited for her to cross the road.

'Hello, Rachel.'

She put on a headlamp smile for me, made me think I was in her good books. 'How do, Doug?'

We planned to head off to the Low Green, but the town was so full of lads carrying carry-outs in that direction that we diverted to Welly Square. It was a fight to find a bench, you just about had to wrestle one from a bloater with a sunburnt torso or a young mum placating a screaming toddler with ice cream.

'This is mental,' said Rachel. She seemed to have mellowed from the cub reporter I'd encountered on my last case. *The Post* was riding high after a string of scoops now, had been through a redesign that had obviously filtered down to the staff.

I started to roll up my shirt sleeves, 'It's twenty-five degrees ... days like that are as rare as hobby horse manure around here.'

'It's almost like summer.' She clawed at the collar of her blouse. 'So, what can I do you for?'

It wasn't a social call, it would be pointless to pretend. I dived in. 'Well, I'm on a case ...'

'Figures.' She leaned back on the bench and tipped her face towards the sky; her sunglasses caught the full glare and shone like flashlights.

Rachel had been good to me in the past but we'd had a connection on that occasion – she knew the victim. I had no *in* with her on this occasion and she'd obviously grown in confidence since our last encounter; I wondered if I wasn't pressing my luck.

'I went through the *Post*'s archives and it's one of your stories.'

'Oh, yeah?'

'Steven Nichols' murder.'

She drew in her lips, moisture glistened on her brow. 'I don't remember that being a premeditated murder. I thought it was just a street fight that went too far.'

'That's what the police say.'

I seemed to have her interest. Rachel leaned forward, sat on the edge of the bench, she was repositioning her sunglasses on the top of her head as she spoke again. 'Are you telling me there's a cover-up?'

Now that I had her attention, I played coy, shrugged my shoulders and looked down the steps of the County Buildings – they looked cool in deep shadow.

Rachel snorted, it was a dismissive gesture. 'Oh, you're so on a fishing trip.'

'Maybe I am, maybe I'm not.' I turned back to face her. 'Are you sure you can afford to rule it out on past form?'

She bit, 'Your form or the police's?'

'Both ...'

Rachel looked around for her bag, found it on the gravel; as she picked it up a dusty plume from the dry-ash ground came with it. 'I'm off, Doug ... good luck with the conspiracy theory. I thought for a moment you might have something useful for me, like an answer to why this town's chock-full of junkies ... nobody seems to have an answer to that.'

We rose together. 'Hang about, just take a look at the lie of the land, that's all I'm asking ... consider it a tip off.'

'We get fees for them in my racket.'

I raised a hand to shield my eyes from the glaring sun. 'You're too young to appreciate deferred gratification, I suppose.'

'Meaning?'

I took a step forward, looked over her shoulder as I spoke. 'My information tells me there could be someone on the force worth looking into.'

Rachel reached up for her sunglasses, lowered them onto her nose and let a sly smile emerge on the side of her face. 'Am I supposed to be tempted by the ring of a police corruption story?'

All that was missing from her demeanour was the head tilted to the shoulder and she would be the picture of sarcastic indifference. I'd seen the look a million times before; my ex-wife wore it every time she knew I was right but didn't want to let on. There was something about her type that wouldn't allow them to change a snap judgement, least it showed weakness.

I played to her. 'Of course, you don't need me to tell you any of this ... a capable hack like yourself can probably clear any suspicion with a couple of phone calls.'

She put her bag on her shoulder and turned away, she was waving to the wide blue sky as she went. 'Goodbye, Doug.'

I hoped I'd done enough to pique her interest; if I hadn't my next move was going to be a lot harder.

Chapter 17

I woke with a line from Burns ringing in my head ...
'The honest man, though e'er sae poor,
Is king o' men, for a' that!'
I knew the reason for it, the valuation on my mother's house had come in the day before. There had been a time when the place was a home, where Claire and I had grown up, but at some point – I don't know when – it had started to be talked of as an asset. We watched the price ascend – two, three, four times what my parents had paid for it. Its current worth was nowhere near those exalted sums and I knew how my sister would react to that.

There was no way I was sitting on the property, waiting and hoping for the market to recover, so I knew my only option was to cut out my share in favour of Claire. She had a family, kids that needed and wanted constantly, I couldn't deny them what we'd had just because the economy had tanked, it seemed beyond unfair, cruel even. And my needs were few, the RUC pension would put a roof over my head, wherever I ended up.

I dragged myself out of bed and wandered down the stairs towards the kitchen. There was a flyer on the mat for the Gaiety Theatre.

'Back in business, eh?' I muttered, managing a rare smile for this hour.

The Gaiety had been a forlorn presence in the town for so long, a visual reminder of its failure that stood proudly proclaiming its presence and vigour that was gleaned from another age. I was delighted to see them back in business; perhaps things weren't so bad after all. Maybe the town was on the up. I turned over the flyer, seemed like the old Gaiety Whirl was coming back too: no Johnnie Beattie this time but a star role for the home-grown talents of one Chris Taylor.

'Good on you, lad.'

The smile, thanks to a shot of good news, lasted all the way to the breakfast bar before I felt my heart sinking once more. I still couldn't get used to the fact that Ben was no longer with us – I was surrounded by memories – even conjured up an old phrase of my father's to capture the tone.

'One swallow doesn't make a summer ...'

I picked up the telephone receiver and dialled Claire's number.

Ringing.

'Hello ...'

She sounded stressed. When did she never?

'Hello, Claire, it's Doug.'

'Doug ... early for you, isn't it?'

'Old habits die hard.' I heard the sounds of shopping bags rustling in the background. 'Is now a good time?'

'I suppose so, what's up?' She sounded tired, strained. She always took on too much.

'I wanted to let you know that I've had the house valued and ...'

She flared, cut in. 'You've what? Surely that's a decision for us to make jointly.'

I always knew the conversation was going to strike a delicate note with Claire, but hadn't foreseen the immediate leap towards fighting talk. Her voice rose, became a cackle, then rose higher yet. She gave me just enough space in the dialogue to mention the price and then the stratosphere didn't seem far enough away to ignore her.

'There's no way ... we'll simply have to wait until the market recovers!'

'Claire, that's not an option ... I'm moving on.'

A loud tut. 'I don't believe this. You've got itchy feet again so we have to suffer.'

I thought her phrasing was a little strong. She hadn't heard me out. 'Look, I'm not going to take a cut, Claire, the proceeds of the house sale are yours to do what you like with.'

She was silenced. The news had thrown her off balance but her voice was still in the clouds. 'I don't believe you.'

'What?'

'Is this some kind of joke?'

'No, Claire ... how could you say that? I want you and your family to have my share.'

A lengthy gap stretched out on the line.

'Claire ... Claire ...'

She'd hung up.

I looked at the phone and flummoxed a response. 'What in the name of ...'

Her reaction had blindsided me. I couldn't believe she would be so petty over something like our dead parent's home. And then I remembered it had been a long time since this place was a home.

A thought occurred to me that Claire might be doing worse than I thought. I remembered my married days – there was never enough money in the pay packet, my wife had always wanted more. Had I let my own life situation creep into this judgement? Had I any right to sell up and move on without my sister's say so? I felt suddenly trapped in the one place I didn't want to be. A tight constriction gripped my chest; I knew what it meant to be trapped ... in a marriage, in a thankless career, literally trapped, with no way out.

I moved over to the sink and opened the window, let some morning air insinuate itself on my face. There was a light dusting of dew on the lawn, a slow bleed of sunrays etching a dark portcullis beyond the fence and wall. At first I didn't even register the figure sitting in one of the patio chairs, slowly drawing on a cigarette. The back was broad, the shoulders square, and not unfamiliar. When he turned to see me at the window he waved quickly, rose and flattened his cigarette underfoot.

I was almost lost for words, but not quite.

'Mason, what on Earth are you doing?'

His steps across the flags were brisk. 'We need to talk, Doug.'

Chapter 18

The sight of Mason greeting me at this early hour T-boned me into despondency – I knew it meant trouble. Maybe the chat with my sister added to it, but either way the result was the same. I watched my friend's bulky movements in my mother's small kitchen and felt the situation was surreal.

'You need to think about getting some security in that garden,' said Mason. 'Some sensor lights at the least ... and a lock on the gate.'

'Don't you think you're preaching to the converted? And anyway, it's going on the market. I'm moving on.'

He didn't reply to my last remark, his face perpetuating a stolid Ayrshire stock, as he sat behind the breakfast bar and pawed at an old copy of the *Post*.

As I poured grey coffee into cups Mason began to snigger, but seemed far from amused.

I took the bait. 'Something tickle your fancy?

He flicked the page of the *Post*. 'This missing parrot story ... I think you missed a trick there.'

I handed over the coffee and sat down in front of him. I'd made the mistake of rising once, I wasn't going to do it again.

'No, I'm serious, Doug ... you being an investigator for hire and all that now.'

He wasn't going to let up. I lowered the cup and fixed him in my glare. 'Let's cut to the chase. What's this about?'

He smiled. 'It's a missing parrot, surely that's within your abilities. You know what a parrot looks like, don't you?'

'Mason, if you've come round to wind me up, I'm in no mood.'

He slammed down the paper. 'Wind you up? Do you think I've got that much time on my hands now that the *Post* are firing questions at the press office on your wild goose – or is that parrot – chase?'

I couldn't hold back a grin, but I seemed to get away with it because Mason thought I was referring to his repartee. My meeting with Rachel hadn't been a total waste of time – she'd stoked the hornets' nest and I could ask no more than that.

I played the innocent. 'Oh, really?'

'Don't come it with me, Doug ... it was the Maciver girl, I know she's one of your contacts.'

He near spat the last word out.

'I think you overestimate me, mate, and maybe underestimate the public feeling on this case. Stevie Nichols was just a young lad, no one likes to see callow youth wasted like that.'

'The case is closed.'

'That what John Scott told you?'

He picked up his cup and started to gulp; his eyes inferred he was swallowing much more anger than coffee. When he stopped, he placed the cup down and silently drummed fingers off his temples. It was a highly affected look, histrionic, and all for my benefit.

'Look, Doug, if you must know I did take a look over the case files ...'

'And ...?' my voice came like a bark.

'And they're sound. There's nothing irregular in the slightest. You've no call to start unpicking John Scott's work.'

The fact that the notes were sound said nothing to me, if I was covering tracks I'd make sure I did a professional job of it and I wouldn't expect a DI of Scott's calibre to do anything else. The fact that they were so clean said more to me than anything else; everything looked and sounded clean cut – too clean cut. I felt the lining of my gut moving.

Mason picked up his cup again, drained the contents and rose. 'So, do you believe me now?'

'Of course. Why would I doubt you?'

He looked surprised, wide whites of eyes on show. 'Well, you being you.'

I smiled, the headshakes which followed were involuntary. 'Mason, do you expect me to go back to that boy's father and say, hand on heart, I've done the best I could?'

Mason's mouth opened, there was a phrase to describe it: catching flies.

'No,' I said, 'I didn't think you would expect me to do that. And why? Because I'm too good a cop, I take pride in my work and I know what I'm doing. This isn't a game to me, it's about justice ... right and wrong, remember those?'

He leaned forward and tapped the newspaper; 'Then get chasing that parrot, or a wife that's playing away from home, a teenage runaway maybe ... Don't be going after decent coppers because you have a wild idea that something doesn't add up. You need more than that to build a case.'

I rose to meet Mason's glare. 'Oh, I know that. I intend to get all the evidence I need.'

His jaw jutted, he spoke through his lower teeth, 'Leave the police work to the professionals, Doug.'

'That's what Bert Nichols did and he's still fallen short on answers.'

He took a step towards the door, gripped a bunch of hair in his hand. 'Do you forget the trouble you caused for the service the last time you got into something like this?'

He used the term *the service* to rattle me, to let me think there'd been some changes since my time. That I was out of my depth. Messing with the big boys. I folded my arms and leaned into the wall, like I was deflecting the notion.

'Mason, my memory's not that short ... and you never know, when I finish up this time, you might be trading that Beamer in for a Jag.'

He turned, put a stare on me. He had a finger raised, the words of a messy lecture hung on his lips, but he somehow found the poise to gather them in.

'You can only kill a sheep once, Doug ... but you can shear it every day. You should remember that.'

He was walking away as my chance to reply escaped me.

Chapter 19

Mason's reaction to the call from Rachel at the *Post* had bemused me at first. I hadn't expected him to immediately re-open the case – or anything like it – but to see him flying to the defence of DI Scott, on such tenuous grounds, was a bit of a shock. I'd seen coppers take to rank with a fervour for the old *noblesse oblige* before, but generally they were younger and a lot less experienced. Mason had quite a few years on the dial and I was sure he knew exactly the way things worked on the force; even if he was calling it the *service* now.

My initial instinct was to dig deeper, get some background on John Scott and see if there was more to my suspicions, but I let it slide. I knew that would be the reactive route and good results rarely followed the pattern of running with your emotions. I'd take my interest in DI Scott a little further later; right now I had a list of names, courtesy of Andy's recent delivery, to look at. And if DI Scott was half the detective he purported to be then he'd already know I was onto him – maybe he'd spare me the bother and come looking for me.

I moved into the living room and put on the television because the silence in the big empty house was getting to me. Jeremy Kyle was on again, blasting some poor lad:

'And what would you have done if the drugs had killed you?' The poor kid didn't even have the marbles to muster a reply. The whole scene made me think about what Rachel had said of the Auld Toun's drug problem – there was no easy answer to where they came from when the whole country was sinking ever deeper into the easy release of oblivion.

I showered and dressed, a fresh pair of 501s and a grey-marl sweat-top. It was a look that said smart but casual, what would once have been referred to as man at C&A, when we still had the big store out front of the Kyle Centre. What a draw for the town that had once been; I managed a smile for happier days Christmas shopping for the cheap clobber I'd get my dad every year: packets of hankies, God-awful shirt and tie combinations in plastic packs held together with a million and one pins; he always smiled and looked grateful but when he went we found a stockpile of them – must have been years' worth – in a sideboard in the garage.

The thought of Dad made me want to call Claire again, try once more to reconnect what little was left of our family ties. I knew if I didn't make the effort to hold onto my last remaining family member, I'd be set adrift. I was at that point in my life where people slipped away from me; old friends I'd lost in the divorce, old family members I'd lost in the passage of time. I looked at the phone, disconsolately perched on the hallway stand, but couldn't summon the strength or gumption to get it. Picking up the phone had once been the easiest thing in the world, even after an argument or rough exchange of words it was not something I'd balk at; but age and a delicate wisdom gleaned from the consequences of my words had started to hold me back. It all seemed like conflict now and I was tired of that. I wanted some peace, I knew that might mean loneliness as well, but I guess that was a set of options I'd have to weigh up when the time came.

In the garden, as I opened up the car I caught sight of a white van pulling up.

'Morning ... Mr Michie, is it?' He looked like a workie, high-vis vest over white T-shirt.

'That's right.'

'I'm from the estate agents, got a for sale sign for you.'

It took me a moment to register what he had said, the accent was Glasgow and required a slight adjustment of the antennae. 'Yeah ... I mean, go ahead.'

He tapped his brow and headed for the back of the van as I got in the Audi and pulled out. I tried not to look at the sign as it emerged from the van, the finality of the transaction was something I still needed a bit of time to deal with.

I'd decided to pay a visit to Steven Nichols' fiancée out Prestwick way. She had a flat on the main drag, across from The Dome – or was it Bonne these days? I could never remember the name of that pub. The little town had almost become subsumed into greater Ayr, only the no man's land of Tam's Brig separating them, but Prestwick seemed to be faring better, much better, than its rival. Trendy bars, cafés and boutiques had sprung up along the road leading into the centre – in all the areas Ayr was failing, Prestwick was thriving. If it had been just a bit further from the Auld Toun I would have put it on my list of possible places to settle.

The notes Andy had gave me directed to a door down from the small-ish supermarket, a Co-op with a side-line in the bunches of flowers I thought only garages sold as peace offerings from late-home husbands.

I took the road down the side of the police station and parked behind the taxi rank. The flat wasn't any more than a five minute walk and there was only two names on the buzzer.

I took out the notes, scanned the names again. 'Milne ... here we go.'

There was a lengthy silence, I thought about pressing the button again, but allowed for the walk to the front of the property.

Static cackles preceded a strangled voice. 'Hello.'

'Hello, I'm looking for Jan Milne.'

I waited for a reply but none came. The door clicked and unhinged itself from the lock. As I took the steps I wondered if she knew who she had let in; perhaps Bert Nichols had told her to expect me.

At the top of the steps a young girl peered round the jamb of the door. 'Who're you?'

'I rang the door ...'

'I know, I thought you were the postie.' Her hair, in tight black curls, was dripping wet. She tightened the neck of her pale-pink dressing gown as she took me in.

'Eh, no ... My name's Doug Michie, I thought perhaps Bert Nichols might have told you to expect me.'

Her face didn't register a flicker. 'No, he didn't.'

'I'm investigating Steven's ... death.'

Her look remained impassive, I sensed a shrug was coming but she didn't move.

'It's not a good time, I'm going out.'

'I'll only take a minute of your time. You and Stevie were engaged, weren't you?'

She rolled eyes; it wasn't the reaction I expected. 'I suppose.'

'Then, if you don't mind, I think you could be a help to me.'

She sighed and retreated into the hallway, the door was widened and a hand gestured me in. It was on the tip of my tongue to remind her that I wasn't selling double glazing, but I didn't want the door slammed on me, which looked a definite possibility.

Chapter 20

I'd taken no more than half a dozen steps into Jan Milne's flat when I noticed a familiar aroma. It was patchouli. When I joined the force one of the seniors I'd been buddied with early in my uniform career had shared some wisdom about patchouli. I could still see Mark Gilchrist's face now – every time I smelled patchouli, it was the same flashback.

'You smell that, Douglas lad?' He always called me by my Sunday name.

'Yeah, think so ... incense, isn't it?'

He grinned on the side of his face, 'Something like that, patchouli it's called and if you ever come across the smell of it on a job again you'll do well to remember one thing ...'

Gilchrist had paused for effect, raised his nose to the air like a bloodhound.

'What's that?' I said.

'The people in the house like to smoke a fair bit of the waccy-baccy ... Either that, or they're the first people I've come across that actually like the smell of patchouli!'

It seemed like a lesson worth storing away; as a masking agent it worked a treat.

Jan took me into the living room, a large, open area with one wall given over to a row of designer kitchen cupboards, a trendy sink and a trendier stove. There were two couches out front – definitely not DFS jobs – and in between them sat a solid-wood coffee table with an ashtray, full to overflowing; Jan made a dash for it as I sat down.

'Sorry, bit of a tip this place today.' She made a weak attempt to cover the distinctive roaches, made from green Rizla packets, with her hand.

I tried to put her at ease. 'It's okay, Jan ... I'm not the police.'

The mention of the word *police* seemed to startle her, she instinctively tucked the ashtray behind her back and changed subject. 'Can I get you a cup of tea?'

I nodded, and as she left I glanced through to the next room: a man's leg dangled from the corner of a double bed; there didn't seem to be any other rooms in the generous flat.

On her way back from the kitchenette, Jan closed the door and then nervously tucked her hair behind an ear as if she was uncomfortable with my presence.

'Been staying here long?' I asked.

She took the half-lit cigarette from her mouth, 'I've every right to be here ... they said I could, the names have been changed over and everything.'

Her defensiveness unsettled me, I sipped my tea slowly and tried again. 'I'm sorry, it must still be quite raw for you. I take it this was Steven's flat?'

She dispersed a blue plume of smoke towards the ceiling. 'No ... I mean yes.'

'Which is it?'

'Stevie rented it but he never stayed here, it's always been my flat.'

I nodded, tried to appear understanding. As I lit my own cigarette she seemed to thaw a little – like anyone who took a cig couldn't be that bad.

'It's on the up, this end of town ...' I said. 'Must be an expensive place to live.'

'It's just a one-bedroom flat.' Her eyes trailed off to the door she'd recently closed as if somehow the mistake was a hanging offence. 'Anyway, I can afford it.'

'That's good to hear. what do you do to pay your way in the world, Jan?'

'I work.'

'Where?'

She huffed, released a long exhalation of cigarette smoke. 'Admin kind of thing.'

'The last I checked admin wasn't paying so well.'

'I get overtime and that ... look, I thought you wanted to ask about Stevie, not me?'

I thought I heard movement in the other room, my gaze followed Jan's earlier trail then returned to her.

'Do you have a visitor?'

'Just a friend.' She stubbed her cigarette in the ashtray, it wasn't finished and snapped in the middle. More sighing followed as she folded her arms and perched herself on the edge of the couch.

'Must be nice staying here, having friends round; did Steven stay too?' I immediately realised my question was more loaded than I intended.

'No, he couldn't stay here. He always went home, it was just a short walk.'

I'd plotted the Nichols' home on the map before I left – it was close, but he'd still have to run the gauntlet of late-night drunks on the main street.

'Was Steven here the night he died?'

She bit her lip. 'Yes.'

'What kind of state was he in when he left?'

'What do you mean?'

'I mean, was he drunk? Stoned? Angry?'

She shook her head, started to play with the cord of her dressing gown. 'None of those, he couldn't go home in a state because his folks would have a fit.'

My tea had gone cold, I put down the cup. 'He was afraid of his parents?'

'Not afraid, just ... it was difficult, they were so controlling.'

I could tell from our first meeting that Bert Nichols was a man of high principles, but I didn't have him down as a martinet and Stevie was old enough to rebel. 'And Steven put up with their controlling?'

She turned away from me, back to the door. There were definite sounds of movement. 'I've told all this to the police, you know.'

'I'm not police,' I reminded her.

Maybe it was the way I said it but she didn't like my mention of the boys in blue. She threw down the dressing gown cord and returned her gaze to me. 'I think he was so used to it that it wouldn't have made a difference if he complained ... but he always said he didn't have a choice. It was the way he'd been brought up, with the religion and that ... his mum and dad don't even smoke or drink, they're just square pegs and wanted him to be the same.'

'Do you think Steven just went along with all this Order stuff to keep his folks happy?'

'Oh, no ...' Her voice rose. 'He was right into all that, him and Davie Grant were best of pals.'

The sound of my employer's name set my head spinning; if there was no love lost between Bert and Davie then it seemed strange – given his parents' tight reins – that Stevie would be bosom buddies with him.

'He was close to Davie Grant?'

She nodded, rapidly. 'Oh, yeah. He worked for him, Davie always said he was a rising star in the company. But I think he always felt he owed his dad for that, y'know, that his dad got him the job. I think he felt a little bit torn, to be honest ...'

As the bedroom door opened a tall twenty-something in skinny jeans and a Superdry T-shirt walked out and as quickly as she had started to open up, Jan signalled the end of the conversation to her guest. 'We're talking about what happened to Stevie ... he's just finishing up.'

The lad flicked a flop of fringe from his eyes and tipped back his head in acknowledgement, then idled his way to the bathroom.

'I'd like you to leave now,' said Jan. She was already on her feet and indicating the door.

Chapter 21

I trooped over to The Dome and stationed myself in the window seat. There were chairs outside, under the awning, but I wanted to keep out of plain sight, for now anyway. I had a clear view of the entrance to Jan Milne's flat and the coffee was good, so I was in no rush to go anywhere. The Dome was one of those places that I remembered from my youth, we'd make a trip up to Prestwick on the long, dark nights and sit around the open fire with pints of Guinness; the place felt exotic then, to a bunch of young lads. The thought that it was likely Steven Nichols' local boozer needled me, he was too young to have died and a life taken so soon always unsettled me, fired my sense of justice.

I wanted to find answers for Bert Nichols and for those that Stevie left behind, but it struck me that his fiancée was already moving on without too much difficulty. Jan wasn't on my list of suspects, though, she was just a daft lassie with too little upstairs to know that others would look at her actions disapprovingly. I didn't fault her – why would I? She was just a kid herself and to expect her to have useful coping mechanisms at her age was unfair, no youngster should have to deal with her burden. The new boyfriend, however, was a mystery to me and I'd have to do some background before I could dismiss him as irrelevant to the case.

I was blowing the froth off my second latte when my iPhone let me know of an incoming text.

It was Lyn.

Sorry to desert you the other day, I'm just in a bad place right now. I thought you might have got back in touch though, but it doesn't matter. I understand ...

I stared at the words and felt a crease forming in my brows. It didn't make any sense until I realised the text sitting above hers, that I'd written the day she left the cafe, hadn't been sent.

'Ouch ...'

I knew at once Lyn was likely to have taken offence but I felt a deepening sense of guilt for having to dig myself out of trouble with her again. She was an old friend, after all, and we'd been through a lot together; she deserved better.

I dialled her number.

Ringing.

'Hello, Doug ...'

I felt relieved she didn't let me go to voicemail. 'Lyn ... look, I'm sorry I didn't contact you sooner.'

'It's okay.'

It wasn't, but she was well aware of that. My tone of voice must have leaked contrition; when people sense that, they know there's no point in rolling out the big guns because the small ones have done their job.

'Would you believe I wrote a text, but didn't send it?' I couched it as a question but she obviously presumed it to be rhetorical and didn't reply. 'How are you now, anyway?'

There was a gap on the line, I glanced down towards Jan's door but there was still no movement.

'Doug, it's fine really. You don't need to back-pedal, I know where I stand now.'

That was it; did she know where she stood? She was my friend and I didn't want to lose that friendship and the combined years we shared in memory. 'Wow, that sounds dramatic.'

'You know me, drama queen to the end!'

I saw a flash of her performing as Lucille in *The Slab Boys* – a Christmas play we'd put on in third year at Ayr Academy. 'Better than my Spanky, anyway!'

A laugh; I'd broken the ice.

'Oh, gawd ... that hair-do.'

'I think it was actually a hair-don't!'

We laughed together, dropped back into the kind of reverie we were better known for, but then the conversation turned to the present day.

'Would you believe I'm in the Dome ... the place hasn't changed much, lick of paint and that but still much as I remember it.'

'I haven't been in there for donkey's years ... they used to do a great Sunday breakfast.'

I could hear the longing in her voice, the call to be somewhere, anywhere other than where she was at the moment. She suffered the existential problem of not being at ease with her own company and for too long life offered very little else for her.

'Well, why don't you join me?'

'Right now?'

'Why not? I'm on a job but it's nothing major, just tidying up a few loose ends.'

Her tone lightened immediately, I could hear the joy return to her voice. 'Are you sure now, Doug? I don't know that many men who can walk and chew gum at the same time.'

'I think I'll manage.'

'Great. I'll just grab the bus, maybe see you in twenty minutes.'

The line died.

As I stared at the phone and cursed myself for failing to send the last text, I felt a creeping anxiety engulf me. I hoped Lyn would understand my offer for what it was and not jump to the conclusion that I'd had a change of heart. As I weighed the thought I knew it was a pointless exercise because people generally let themselves believe what they want to, especially when they're feeling at the low end of the human emotional scale. Lyn even had form for it, convincing herself that two wrongs made a right if it meant she was at least perceived to be happy, in a relationship, settled.

I gulped the last dregs of my coffee. As I put the cup back on the saucer the door to Jan's flat opened and she stepped out with her new man. She was dressed in typical office attire, a navy skirt, white blouse and a black leather jacket tucked over the crook of her elbow; her new bloke hadn't changed.

They were walking towards the bar, not quite hand in hand but exchanging intimate glances and nudges. When they came level with the window I focussed the phone's camera at them and clicked away. I had three or four good, clean shots by the time they turned down the street next to the newsagents and got into a pimped-up metallic blue Clio. I snapped the back end of the car, number plate and all, just for good measure.

'Bingo,' I muttered under my breath as I watched the car speeding off.

Chapter 22

What was the old phrase? Something like, *Man plans, God laughs* ... As I woke up and stared at Lyn's head on the pillow next to mine I knew we'd crossed a boundary neither of us had foreseen; well, certainly I hadn't.

She was sleeping, her long dark hair sweeping her bare shoulders. It felt wrong to stare; I turned away and took in the carnage of the room. The abandoned clothes, the upturned bottle of Absolut and the messy remnants of the Royal Blossom's take-away containers.

My eyes drew me back to Lyn; she seemed to be smiling in her sleep, content. There was a response queuing on my lips, something like, 'Oh, sweet Lord ...' but I held schtum and backed out of the bed.

I scooped up my clothes from the floor; I seemed to be missing a shoe but presumed it couldn't be too far away. As I closed the door and dressed in the hallway, my gut turned, acid bile making its way up my windpipe. It could have been the food, I told myself, but a siren wail inside my head begged to differ.

'Vodka ...' I was at the age where social drinking meant a bottle of wine, maybe a tot of Tia Maria under the tinsel at Christmas time. What was I playing at?

The missing shoe showed itself on the top step of the

staircase. I carried the pair all the way to the kitchen, presuming my stockinged feet would be best not to wake my guest. I scrunched my eyes at the thought of Lyn lying in my bed, but the image wouldn't dissolve. I tried to ask myself what I was doing, why had this happened? I was moving on and Lyn was looking for something I couldn't offer, or didn't want. Well, that had been my last rational assumption.

In the kitchen I opened the window and hoped my frayed nerves would negotiate for peace with the first cigarette of the day. The hangover I could just about live with, but the guilt trip was the killer. I'd fallen for Lyn before and had the idea blow up in my face. I'd been on the rebound from my failed marriage and Lyn looked like the answer to my misery. At least, that's what I thought at the time; looking back now I think it was more a case of like attracting like. She was at a low ebb then, too, and saying our goodbyes had been the right thing to do. It was a period in my life I'd tried to bury, move on from, move away from ... at best, I'd allow myself to resort to the wisdom of Burns.

Had we never lov'd sae kindly,
Had we never lov'd sae blindly,
Never met — or never parted –
We had ne'er been broken-hearted.

The kettle was boiling when I heard the door creak behind me. Lyn appeared in the doorframe with bed head and bare legs, smiling. The sight of her awake, and clearly cognisant, kicked something inside me.

'Good morning ...' I said.

As she walked towards me the bare soles of her feet slapped the cold floor. She put her arms round my neck and tucked her head into my shoulder. It seemed the most natural thing in the world to do the same, so I did, but something told me it wasn't an act without consequence.

We drank tea and discussed the possibility of breakfast, we even managed to look at a loaf of bread and contemplate toast, but declined. The awkward feeling between us faded but didn't subside. It was as if there was a great question hanging in the air around us. Of course, neither of us were naive enough to say the words 'what now?' That was for teenagers or commitment addicts; both of us had been around the block far too many times to countenance such a gauche move. We talked about the weather, Ayr United's parlous financial affairs and just about anything that filled the silent gaps.

'Are you going to put your shoes on?' said Lyn.

'I suppose I should.' I collected the worn brogues from the barstool beside me. 'They've seen better days, I'll have to take them to Blaney Quinn.'

Lyn's dark eyes lit, 'Eh, I don't think so ...'

The Auld Toun's oldest cobbler had been rumoured to be on the verge of retirement for twenty years now. 'Don't tell me he's shut up shop.'

Lyn grimaced, showed an inverted smile. 'You didn't hear?'

'Hear what?'

'I'm afraid he did retire ... and then passed away really quickly after.'

The news didn't seem real; I'd have believed Markies had slipped into the River Ayr first. 'That's too sad for words.'

'I loved that wee place.'

'Everybody did.'

The conversation seemed suddenly gravid with our own mortality. I wanted to change tack; my instinct was to talk of my desire to leave Ayr, get away from all the memories –

good and bad – and start afresh. But that wasn't an option.

Lyn took the lead. 'Have you sent me those pictures yet?'

She was talking about the shots I'd taken of Jan Milne and her boyfriend. Lyn's son was about the same age as them – she thought he might recognise the lad.

'Er no, I'll do that now ...' I took my iPhone from the pocket of my Levi's; Lyn snatched it out my hand and scrolled to the pictures.

'He looks familiar.'

'I thought that too.'

'What are you saying, all boys that age look alike?'

I nodded. 'Well, look at the get-up ... skinny jeans and a Rollers' haircut.'

Lyn frowned and handed me back the phone. 'Send me the pictures, I'll get Glenn to have a look at them. This is a small town, you know what it's like, the young ones all know each other.'

It struck me she was right, it also struck me that her son might have had some knowledge of the victim, too. 'Did Glenn know Steven Nichols?'

'He knew of him, I remember him commenting that he was a flashy sort when the news came out.'

'Aren't they all flashy at that age? The lad in the pic has a Clio that must cost an arm and a leg to insure, let alone keep on the road.'

She rose, collected a towel from a pile on the worktop, and walked towards the kitchen door. 'Doug Michie, I think your opinions are hardening faster than your arteries ... loosen up.'

She had a point, neither of us were remotely flashy at that age; the thought was a further realisation of just how far back we really went.

I waved her off. 'The shower's at the top of the stairs ... make yourself at home, why don't you.'

Chapter 23

The house had never looked so tidy. I couldn't ever recall my mother using Glade plug-ins, but then, towards the end she was lucky to rise out of bed and attach herself to a bottle. I'd grown used to the grey dusting of fluff that covered the living room carpet and almost registered the shape of my footfalls on my rare forays in there, but the new brightness of the pile almost assaulted my eyes.

'I had to empty the bag twice ... when did you last run a hoover over this room?' said Lyn.

A shrug was my best answer. 'I'm not the world's greatest housekeeper.'

'You've got that right.' She sallied off towards the kitchen, and likely some more chores.

I rolled my eyes to the ceiling as she went; it wasn't that I didn't appreciate her help – especially now the house was on the market – but there was something that felt wrong. I trailed Lyn through to the kitchen.

'You know, just because I'm handless in here doesn't mean you have to pick up the slack ...' I said.

She turned and stuck out her hip, 'Don't I know it, sunshine!' She placed a hand on her jutting hip, as if for dramatic effect. 'I'm not doing it for you, it's because I don't like living in a pig-sty.'

She turned and went back to the sink, flicked the taps on nearly to full. There was one word in her speech that was stuck in my head like a bad tune – *living*. I tried to tell myself it was no more than a turn of phrase, a grasp for words, but there was no denying that there was a heavier connotation. If I'd been a bit surer of myself, or a bit less aware of Lyn's feelings, I'd have jumped on the statement and tried to make something of it, had it out with her. The fact of the matter was I'd reached a point in my life where my main purpose had become getting through each day without upsetting anyone – even if it meant storing up trouble for myself.

'Are you still here?' said Lyn. She turned around, started to push her fingers into a pair of yellow Marigold gloves; the rubber snapped tight.

'I'm just leaving.'

She went back to the taps. 'Do you want me to get something in for tea?'

My heart froze. Had we become so settled already? She'd been here no more than a couple of days and already we sounded domesticated.

'Well, I suppose.' I tried to deflect the suggestion, move the arrangement back onto a more temporary affair. 'Or I can bring back a pizza.'

'Forget it! That wheelie bin out there's stuffed with pizza boxes, is that what you've been living on?'

I gripped my rapidly inflating spare tyre, 'I suppose I've got used to not cooking.'

'Well, it's changed days, Doug Michie ... soon as I've cleaned that oven I'm heading to the shops – steak pie do you? Pollock Williamson at the bottom of the town do a great steak pie.'

I watched her retrieve the stainless-steel shelves from the oven and start to wrestle them into the sink. She seemed content, happier than I'd seen her in weeks. I knew it wasn't the idea of cleaning up after me, so that only left one option; I dared not think about how I was messing with her head, or if my own bonce could cope either.

I set off for the front door, collected my old black leather from the coat-stand; it was a waist-length job that I'd had for years but had hardly worn because my ex-wife had called it my 'bouncer's coat'. She thought I looked like a doorman in the jacket but the days of her thoughts having the slightest influence on me were well and truly over.

I collected the car keys and headed out.

The Audi started on the first turn of the ignition, by the Loaning the engine was purring sweetly. I was on my way back out to Prestwick, to pay an unannounced visit to Bert Nichols and try to divine some information about his son's former fiancée. Something Jan Milne had said about the Nichols being God-botherers made me wonder just who I was dealing with. Turning the other cheek and tolerance didn't seem to be regular hits on the Order's radar so Bert's enthusiastic involvement was puzzling. Still, he wouldn't be the first religious hypocrite I'd come across – in Ulster they were ten a penny.

I'd reached Wallacetown, was taking the roundabout at Waggon Road, when I spotted a Mondeo speeding up behind me. I ventured as far as the Prestwick Road when I noticed the blue lights flashing in the Mondeo's grille.

'What in the ...?'

I tried to check out the driver, to see if it was a face I knew, but the sun visor was down. A finger at the end of a flailing arm started pointing me into the side of the road.

'Okay ... okay.'

I pulled in, stilled the engine. As I waited for the flashing blue lights to subside I eyed the Mondeo driver. I still couldn't see a face, but the broad shoulders and the collar and tie told me it was a bloke.

'Come on, show yourself ...'

The lights died and a door opened. For a moment a thought occurred to me that it might be an old colleague on the wind up, but the short stocky frame didn't ring any bells. As the face hove into view I saw there was a beard attached, a thin straight nose and dark eyes above which kept watch on my movements at the wheel. The figure moved swiftly, decisive footing on the busy road, unmoved by the speeding traffic and the soundings of horns by those inconvenienced by him parking across the junction.

As the police officer reached my car window he cracked a heavy knuckle on the glass, rapping impatiently.

I opened up.

I knew at once the face staring back at me. It belonged to the inscrutable DI John Scott.

Chapter 24

I have to be honest and say that the sight of DI Scott at the window of my motor wasn't a pleasant one. He was slightly out of breath but hadn't been running so I put that down to either poor cardio fitness or a simmering anger – the fleshy folds above his beard seemed flushed too, white radial lines breaking at the corners of his eyes.

'Doug Michie,' he said, more like a question than a statement.

'I take it you don't want to see my drivers' licence if you know who I am.'

He leaned over, drummed fingers on the roof of my car. 'I was thinking it was time you and me had a chat ... what do you say?'

I looked ahead, shrugged. 'What about?'

He palmed the roof, but didn't answer my question. 'Turn the car around, follow me up, eh?'

'Okay ... lead the way.'

I turned the key in the ignition.

DI Scott took the road back into Ayr; he seemed to be heading for the centre of town, but at the King Street roundabout took the road ahead and swung round past the college.

'Where are you taking me, *Detective Inspector*?' I

mouthed the words under my breath; if he thought he was driving me out to the wilds for a meeting with his night-stick, he could think again.

At the next roundabout he did a U-turn, swung under the railway bridge and made for the underground car park at Debenhams. He either wanted to chat in the subterranean seclusion or he was perfectly content to keep our meeting in the open.

As Scott's Mondeo parked up, I pulled alongside and lowered my window.

He yelled to me across the cold expanse of concrete, 'I'll buy you a coffee, you know the Costa?'

I nodded, but couldn't quite believe what I was hearing. Scott seemed to want to recreate the Pacino and De Niro scene from *Heat*; I could almost see him telling me if I got in his way he was taking me down. The thought forced a smirk onto my face.

'Something funny?' he said.

'No, nothing at all ... let's get this coffee.'

In Costa we took a small table towards the rear of the café; we were parallel to the counter and the serving staff – full view of all the goings on.

Scott returned with a tray, two large cups on top, and a *Glasgow Herald* folded beneath his arm. 'You're probably wondering why I picked this place?'

'Not really.'

'Well, it's because it's busy ... and out in the open.' He put down the tray and the newspaper.

'And that's how you want it.'

He nodded. 'That's how I want it, Mr Michie ... all out in the open, no funny business ...'

I cut him off. 'And no funny handshakes.'

He didn't reply to my prodding, but he registered a change of expression that said I knew he was a member of the Craft. My most recent experience with that section of the police service had taught me that there was no need for subtlety where they were concerned.

'I hear you've been ... investigating me, Mr Michie.'

'Please, call me Doug ... makes me think I owe you money when you put the honorific in there.'

His smile showed a flash of teeth in the opening of his heavy facial hair. 'You don't dispute it, then ... Doug?'

I lowered my coffee cup, 'Why would I?'

'Well, I'm glad we can talk frankly. You'll understand why I want to ask a frank question – why?'

'If you know I'm interested in you, I'm sure you'll know why.'

A woman started to raise her voice over at the cake counter, yelling at a young boy who was struggling to decide on the empire biscuit or the custard slice. Scott turned towards the outburst, spoke; 'I've done some homework on you myself.' He turned back to face me. 'Made quite a name for yourself in Ulster ... and in the old home town recently.'

Did I want to play tit for tat with him? The answer was no. I presumed he had more to lose in this exchange than me, unless he had something different to say. I laid out my cards. 'Look, John, you know I'm looking into the death of Steven Nichols, so why don't you just come out and say it?'

It was his turn to take another sip of coffee, the conversation was becoming punctuated with these pauses. 'I thought you were calling it a murder?' He made sure not to have eye-contact with me when he said the word.

'That would be putting the cart before the horse, don't you think? Making an assumption and then going looking for the evidence to back it up doesn't sound like good detective work, does it?'

The same rictus of a smile appeared in his beard again. 'And that's what you think you're doing ...' The smile evaporated. 'The case is closed, or do you doubt the work of your former colleagues, Doug?'

The remark was either concentrated sarcasm or a veiled threat, I couldn't quite figure which because Scott's facial expression, hidden behind the beard, didn't give much away. 'The official investigation might be closed, but mine isn't.'

'What makes you think you'll come to any different conclusions?'

'Oh, come on ... it's all a bit convenient, the lad being stabbed by an unnamed and untraceable assailant, don't you think?'

'No.' The answer came flatly. 'And if you'd reviewed the case, a man of your undoubted experience, I'm sure you'd agree.'

He started to get up from the table, he loosened the tie around his meaty neck and stretched out his shoulders like he'd just completed a long journey.

'What's that supposed to mean?' I said.

He leaned onto the table, tapped on the cover of the *Herald* he'd put down earlier. 'I was going to have a look and see if they did a write up on the Ayr game ... good paper for sports, the *Herald*.' He moved away from the table's edge and headed for the door; if there was a goodbye then I missed it, my focus being on the newspaper in front of me.

As the door closed I turned over the paper, sitting inside was the unmarked plastic casing of a CD.

'Well, well,' I said. 'Isn't life full of surprises.'

Chapter 25

I picked up the CD and put it in my pocket, for the millionth time I told myself not to expect the obvious when life had a way of delivering the opposite. I headed out of Costa and back to the car park lift in Debenhams, all the while my thoughts whorling with what could be contained on the shiny little piece of plastic.

Back underground, the columnar concrete grid seemed to confuse me for a moment; added to the stale air and strange echoing of dim sounds off the walls, I struggled to find my bearings. A dizzy rush filled my head at the thought of what had just happened because none of it felt real; nothing did anymore.

The car door hissed closed and I pressed my head into the seat. I took a few minutes just to gather my composure and then I removed the CD and tried it in the player; the disc receded slowly, slid back out.

'Must be data ...'

I stored the disc in the glovebox and tried not to let my imagination get the better of me. Whatever it was that DI Scott had delivered, it would give up its secrets soon enough; speculating wasn't going to expedite the process.

There was no sign of the DI's car as I headed back onto the street, I kept an eye on the rear-view mirror for a little while, just in case he had decided to keep tabs on me, but he didn't show. There was a point during my service in Ulster that I became obsessive about being followed and having the unsettling feeling return made my shoulders tense.

I parked up in one of Welly Square's angled-parking slots and removed the disc. I headed for the print shop over the road from the bus station, which had some computer access. The man on the till nodded to me as I selected a terminal and started to get down to business. My fingertips were sticky, my palms hot, as I slotted in the disc; it didn't take long to display one document icon on the screen.

I clicked it open.

The document was a facsimile, seemed to have been printed and then scanned. It was on official police paper, the type I knew only too well. I scrolled further, there were lots of documents: an incident report; witness statements; post-mortem results.

'The file ...' It looked like Scott had copied the complete police incident file from the Steven Nichols case and simply handed it over to me.

I couldn't believe my luck at first, and then I started to wonder why.

'Excuse me, mate ... can I print from here?'

The man at the till pointed to a free-standing printer. 'Yeah, will come out there.'

I set the file to print; the pages started to stack-up on the other side of the room.

From even the most cursory scroll through the pages I could tell Scott had been thorough; nothing had been left out. Every 't' had been crossed; every 'i' dotted. It felt like an exercise in grandstanding – a case of look how professional I am, how could you doubt my findings? It would take closer scrutiny to turn up anything I could use; as the printer wheezed to a halt, I paid up and headed back to the car.

Tony Black

I found myself driving to clear my head. I was going nowhere in particular, just looking to release some throttle, gun the engine into that reassuringly hypnotic sound that lulled you out of grim reality. One second I thought of the case and just why DI Scott would hand over the file, unbidden, when even Mason was averse to that kind of patter. The next second my mind rushed onto my domestic situation and how to solve it, but neither stream of thought delivered answers.

On the shore I realised I'd circuited the town like a boy racer. I stopped for a while, watching the dark sea, still and silent, soughing against the port walls. Occasionally a spill of sand erupted from the beach path and started to chase the litter. The minutes sauntered along in fine style until I realised all I was achieving in my distraction was avoiding returning home.

Before Lyn had installed herself in my parents' house I hated the thought of returning to the empty, lonely existence I had there. Now, I avoided the place with the same enthusiasm but for a different reason. I knew, at some deep level, I was probably afraid of having my feelings bruised again. But, perhaps more than anything, I was afraid of upsetting Lyn when she'd clearly been through enough.

The westering sun was cutting a red welt across the evening when I finally pulled up at the house. The small table lamp in the living room window was on, something I hadn't seen for years. I knew Lyn was inside, likely slaving over a hot stove, but there was something about the picture that unsettled me more than usual. As I got out the car and made my way towards the front door I could hear voices coming from the house. I turned the handle on the door and went inside – narrowed the chatter down to two females – both of whom I recognised.

Disbelief was the primary emotion swirling inside my

head as I walked into the living room and set eyes on Lyn and the back and shoulders of the woman sitting beside her.

'Oh, hello ...' said Lyn. 'Look who's here!'

She seemed chipper, her words a skilled glissade reserved for social niceties; they couldn't have been more misdirected on this occasion.

'You?' I spat the word as my chest began to tighten. I couldn't believe the scene before me.

My sister's gaze traced the line of the ceiling and then fell sharply to the floor as she sprung from her seat and placed a polite peck on my cheek.

'Hello, Doug ... I bet you weren't expecting to see me so soon.'

Chapter 26

This day was turning out to be full of surprises. As I stood before Lyn and my sister in the living room I felt momentarily lost for words – lost for a lot more besides if I was to tell the truth.

Lyn clasped her hands together, spoke: 'Right, well, I think I'll go and make some tea.' She was smiling as she left us, delicately enclosing my sister and me in a private pow-wow.

'She seems to have her feet under the table,' said Claire.

I breathed deep but stifled the urge to sigh. I knew I was being tested, I could handle that, but the next level on the dial I wasn't so sure about. 'She's trying to be nice,' I said, then, changing the subject. 'I didn't see your car outside.'

'I came on the train. We only have the one car now, it's too expensive to run two.' Claire's answer was curt, a broadside signalling her intentions. 'But I'm sure you're not interested in my travel arrangements, Doug.'

I couldn't stop my gaze rolling away from her and around the room, desperate for something less painful for it to alight upon.

Claire pulled me back into her ambit. 'Is she staying here?'

'Her name's Lyn.'

'Oh, I know she has a name.' The remark was calculated to be interpreted any way I wanted. Claire could turn on the bitchiness like a tap when she needed to; it wasn't her usual state, far from it, but when she felt boxed in she became belligerent. I knew this because it was a family trait that I kept in my own locker.

'Look, Claire, you've nothing to fear from Lyn.'

My sister folded her arms, huffed. 'No, not much ...' She paused for a moment then unfastened her hand and pointed a sharp fingernail at me. 'Do you think I came up the Clyde on a biscuit, Doug? I know what's going on here.'

She was edging dangerously close to venting. For years we'd batted our frustrations with the outside world off these walls and at each other, but I thought that time had long passed. We were adults now, we had lives of our own beyond silly sibling rivalry. The issue at hand wasn't who got the family saloon on the weekend, or whose turn it was to take the school trip; we were beyond all that, surely.

'Claire, sit down ...' I reached out an arm and she flicked it away. 'Please, Claire.'

My sister turned away from me and went to the front of the room where she stood staring out of the window. 'I just can't believe what you're doing here, Doug.'

My palate dried over, I pressed my tongue on to the roof of my mouth in an effort to activate some salivary glands. I knew what I wanted to say to her, and how I wanted to say it, but was also grateful my anxiety was keeping a check on it.

Claire's voice rose, 'I mean, shacking up with some random ...'

I cut in. 'Shut up.'

She turned, her mouth drooped open. I didn't give her a chance to reply.

'Just listen to yourself will you ...'

105

The door handle moved behind us as Lyn pushed into the living room carrying a tray, balancing cups and a teapot. She looked on edge, her eyes moving quickly as she spoke. 'Well, here's the tea, I'm sure you could do with a cuppa after the trip, Claire. I'm not going to join you both. I have a few things to do in town, so will let you catch up together.'

She hurried out the room, avoiding all eye contact. I hoped to hell she hadn't heard Claire earlier and I could tell by the way my sister crooked her head that she felt the same way.

When the front door closed, Claire spoke. 'Do you think she heard me?'

There didn't seem any point in making matters worse for her. 'I doubt it, she's just giving us our space, she knows we need to talk.'

Claire brushed her upper arms with the palms of her hands and sucked in her bottom lip; it was a remorseful look. 'I don't want to get at Lyn.'

'I know.'

'I mean, I like Lyn, we all went to the Academy together ...'

'Claire, you don't need to explain.'

'But, Doug, you have to see this from my point of view,' her tone started to rise again. 'I mean, first you announce out of the blue that you're selling up and next thing you're moving her in! I mean, just what's going on?'

I turned towards the tray, made a fuss of pouring out the tea and stirring in the milk. I noticed there were little triangular sandwiches, cheese and ham, but my appetite deserted me. I passed Claire a cup. 'The two incidents aren't related, in any way.'

My sister frowned, painted a disbelieving smirk on her face. 'Please, credit me with some intelligence ...'

I took my cup over to the chair my father used to sit in

and lowered myself onto the seat. 'Claire, coming back here was a bad move for me. I thought it would give me some kind of context, after all that had happened in Ulster ...'

She prompted me. 'But ...'

'But it really only gave me a place to hide. I can't stay here, if I do it's like I'm in retreat from the future, don't you see that? I'm moving backwards instead of forwards.'

Claire looked into her teacup and fell silent. She seemed to be digesting my words.

'I know the market's not good right now, Claire. We might get more if we hold on, but life's too short, surely.'

She looked up, her eyes seemed moist. 'You were never one to hold back were you?'

'*Meaning*?'

'Meaning, it's always been about what you want. Off and away at the drop of a hat, chasing rainbows and the like, and now you're back telling me you need another adventure.' She gripped the cup tightly. 'I did all the right things, Doug. I settled for what I could get, I stuck with it. We might not have much in Inverness, but we got there playing by the rules.'

I didn't understand why she was targeting me. 'Are you blaming me for your choices?'

'No!' She rose, stood in front of me. 'But you must see how unfair it is. I have a mortgage and kids and a husband with no prospects of ever advancing in a career he's worked hard at for years ... this house, this inheritance, is all I have to make the sums add up, Doug.'

I understood where she was coming from; neither of us were ever going to have the kind of security our parents had from this life. I knew it, felt sore about it, but I also knew as a parent it created much more misery for her.

'Look, Claire, I told you I don't want anything from the house sale.'

'I can't let you do that.' She was forceful, adamant, her blurred eyes suddenly sharpening on me.

'Well, what else can I do, Claire?'

She stepped towards me, 'Don't sell up. Just ride out this recession a bit longer, wait and see if the market recovers ... this is all we have, Doug, all we'll ever have.'

My sister stared deep into me, I could feel her gaze burrowing inside me for the answer she wanted. If I refused her then I'd lose my last link to family, to normalcy, in this world. But if I stayed, I was a good as dead.

Chapter 27

I dropped Claire off at the train station and parked up at the far end, overlooking the track. I watched the Glasgow Central train pulling out and wished, somehow, that I was on it. My sister had kept her farewells on the down-low; I'd usually pass her a couple of quid to get the nippers some sweets but raising the spectre of money didn't seem the thing to do.

If I was being the selfless adult I knew I should be then I'd withdraw the house from the market and leave it at that. But the deep sense of soul-weariness the thought created inside me said it wasn't an option. I could live with keeping the house on, maybe renting it out – after all, I wasn't going to profit from it. But I knew the real reason I didn't want to keep it was because of the ties it represented to my past – I wanted out of Ayr, I couldn't be on hand to play the landlord's role every time a pipe burst or the guttering blew away. I wanted a fresh start; at my age, there weren't going to be too many of those coming along.

I walked down the High Street, heading towards the Bridge's Bar. I texted ahead to confirm Andy was in residence and he replied in the affirmative. It was time to put this case on the front foot, though after reading further into the files DI Scott had provided, I knew I was more than likely to put a few people on the back foot. After going through the files I felt more involved than ever – was it the fact that the case provided a distraction from my current home life? Maybe. But there was also the fact that, perhaps for the first time, I could see the shapes coming together at the end of the kaleidoscope.

I shouldered into the door at Bridge's, seemed to bring too much light into the place, the crowd of bar-flies greeted me with squinting eyes.

'God, it's like a vampire's pit in here!' I smirked to the assembled.

'Have you a stake? ... and garlic?' said Andy.

'Do I look like Jamie Oliver?'

He slapped my stomach, 'Few more pizzas and you won't be far off.'

I put a stare on him and ordered a fresh round. We retreated towards the rear of the pub. The tables were empty, the years of carvings – initials and band names mainly – stood out as the sun crept down from the back window.

'Look, Simple Minds,' said Andy.

'Great band ...'

He pointed with his finger to the delicate engraving that had been there long enough to gather a colouring darker than the wood's patina. I could hear Jim Kerr belting out *Alive and Kicking* inside my head, it transported me back to a time and place where things were much simpler. It also conjured up an image of Lyn in her younger days, pogoing at the Piv, for some reason. She was wide-eyed and gallus, smiling like a starlet; it had been so long since she looked that way I felt the image about to fell me.

'What's up?' said Andy.

'Oh, nothing ...'

'You look like you've seen a ghost.'

I shook off the suggestion, lest it led to further probing.

I reloaded with my new ammunition, hoping to catch Andy off guard.

'I got hold of the police files for Steven Nichols' case.'

'What?' It didn't sound like a question.

'Makes for some interesting reading.'

Andy leaned forward, balanced on his elbow. 'I bet it does.'

I let him hang for a moment, took a sip from my pint of mild. 'There's something I've wanted to ask you, right from the start I've noticed something ...'

'What's that?'

'Grantie and Bert ... they're never together.'

'So?'

'So, Andy, what I want to know is ... why?'

He slouched back in his seat, looked speculative then shrugged. 'I have no idea.'

'Oh, come on now ... it wouldn't be because they're at each other's throats now, would it?'

Andy took a deep breath, fidgeted on his seat; his agitated manner told me all I needed to know.

'Don't answer, then ...' I said. 'By that, I mean you don't need to, your face says it all.'

He tried to claw some ground back. 'Well, I don't suppose it's any secret that the pair of them don't really see eye to eye, personally like ... in terms of the Order they're well and truly on the same page.'

I'd had my doubts before about Grant, simply because in Ayrshire, big men liked to throw their weight around. 'And what if, say one time, this animosity spilled over ...'

Andy creased his nose, showed the palms of his hands. 'I don't know what you're saying?'

'Well, then, let me make it black and white for you.' I produced a page from the police file, just one page, with one highlighted paragraph where DI John Scott had listed a possible suspect with a possible motive for the murder of Steven Nichols.

Andy read slowly, his lips tracing the words as he struggled to take in what the page said. 'I don't believe it.'

'It's all written down there ... the police had your old mate Grantie in the frame.'

'But ... how? I mean, why?'

'I suppose we'd really need to ask DI Scott for an explanation to that one ... But before we take that step I think we should put the question to Mr Grant himself, don't you think?'

Andy's face lit, 'Oh, come on ... he won't like that.'

'Won't like what? Being asked if he's a murderer or why the hell he's hired me to investigate a case that's going to put him on the suspect's list for a second time?'

The colour drained from Andy's cheeks, he seemed to be losing the original flush of anger. His breathing slowed, then stilled as he picked up his pint and started to drain the glass.

'Aye, you better drink up, mate. We've got people to see.'

Chapter 28

Summer rain shadowed us out to Dalmellington. What was normally a bleak stretch of road became bleaker with each tick of the odometer. Grey-to-black clouds flanked us, threatening a heavier downpour over expectant fields.

'We'll have had our summer then,' said Andy.

'We just about got a whole week of it this year, you complaining?'

'No, no ... any more and we'd be in the record books.'

Andy's banter verged on forced, the kind of formal chatter reserved for car journeys and enclosed spaces. We had things to discuss, but the tight confines of our enforced union didn't seem the place. I flicked on West FM and let the DJ regale us both with a round-up of the region's holiday highlights. Craig Tara, out on the coastal road at the foot of the Carrick hills, was still doing a turn – the name change from Butlin's fooling no one. I couldn't see myself putting down hard-earned cash on a trip to the place: water slides and the like were for families; the thought prompted a return to images of my sister and her kids. I knew I couldn't afford to lose the last connection I had to family and the real world, but the pull to escape Ayr was still strong.

As I turned into Davie Grant's driveway, the house looked quiet, almost empty.

'Think he's out?' I said.

Andy shrugged. 'That Cassie one will be – bit of rain won't stop her, she's a shop till you drop if ever I saw one.'

I parked up on the gravel drive beyond the front door and stilled the engine. As I got out I glanced over to Andy – caught him nervously smoothing the sides of his mouth with his long fingers.

'Everything okay?' I said.

He didn't answer. I prompted again, 'Andy ... you alright?'

He squared his shoulders. 'Aye, come on, let's get this over with.'

We approached the door, set the bell chiming and waited. I watched Andy's Adam's apple rise and fall as he prepared himself for Grantie's appearance.

'You know, you can wait in the car if you'd sooner not come in,' I told him.

'It's fine.' He glanced at me, thinned eyes glowering, 'I said I'd come and here I am.' I cut Andy some slack in the situation – we were about to hit his friend with an uncomfortable accusation – I didn't envy Andy's position.

A rattle of locks and chains began behind the door in the small smoked-glass window we could see the familiar bulk of Grantie moving. When the door opened he stood before us like a nightclub bouncer waiting to tell us 'not tonight, lads'.

'Hello again,' I said.

Grantie didn't answer, turned to Andy as if he was looking for an explanation for this downright impertinence.

Andy spoke. 'Got a bit of an update for you ... on the case.'

'Oh, aye.' He didn't seem interested, his mouth tightening into a tiny knot, then: '... I suppose you better come in.'

Grantie's gaff had less of an impact on me the second time round, though I found myself clocking Andy's shambling movements as he manoeuvred himself, hunched and tense, around the palatial setting. He looked like an uninvited guest at a funeral, someone that had blagged his way in for a free sandwich.

Grantie directed us to the same seating area as the last time. He was curt, perfunctory in his hospitality. I waited to be offered a drink but none came this time.

'So, what's all this about?' he said.

Andy glanced out the window so I stepped up to the plate.

'There's been some developments, Mr Grant.'

He shrugged in his seat, leaned back as if to project disinterest. 'I don't need a running commentary, unless you've found Stevie's killer, then a phone call would have done.'

I shook my head, made sure my gaze was steel. 'No, I don't think so, not this time; you see I've managed to get hold of some very interesting information in the form of the official police report.'

Grantie looked at Andy, then back to me. 'Oh, yes. Interesting reading was it?'

'Very ...' I watched Grantie for any poker tells, but none came. 'Why didn't you inform me you were a suspect?'

'I don't like to spoon feed people I'm paying to do a job.'

'You must have known I'd find out, though.'

'And what relevance would it have to the outcome, Mr Michie?'

Answering my questions with more questions of his own wasn't going to get us anywhere. I upped the ante with a direct shot across his bows; 'Did you just hire me to get you off the hook?'

He stood up, 'Now hold on, son ...' Grantie tapped his chest with a heavy finger, 'I *am* in the clear.'

I watched our host walk towards the sideboard on the back wall and start to pour himself a drink. He didn't offer to share.

'I hired you to put that family's mind at rest, because we look after our own here and ...' he returned to the sofa and lowered himself down, 'and nothing else.'

I knew he was lying, after a lifetime on the force I didn't need to hear the words. I toyed with the idea of asking him – if the Order was so keen on looking after its own – then why would Bert Nichols tip me off to DI Scott's investigation? But I didn't rate my chances of a straight answer, and anyway, his reaction had told me all I needed to know.

'Are you sure it was Bert's mind you wanted to put at rest and not his mouth?'

'What? Just what's that supposed to mean?'

I allowed myself half a grin at his reaction. 'It means that maybe Bert had some cards of his own to play and he could create trouble for you and your organisation.'

Grantie quaffed a fair share of his drink, it seemed to still his temper. 'I run a very tight ship and I certainly don't allow anyone, even Bert Nichols, to undermine me.'

'Is that what he did – try to undermine you?'

'No. You're putting words in my mouth, Michie, and I won't have that. Don't forget who's paying your way here.'

I knew to quit when I was ahead. And there was nothing to gain from getting him riled, yet. I rose from my seat and headed for the door, motioning Andy to follow.

'I'll be in touch, Mr Grant,' I said.

I heard Andy scuffling behind me, he sounded like a half-scared rat deserting a sinking ship.

Chapter 29

The rain ceased its heavy percussion on the car roof by
the time we hit the A77. Andy eschewed all speech, rested
his head on the high-backed seat like the still corpse of
a man lain in state. We settled into the drive in silence,
accompanied only by the dull thrum of the Audi's engine
and the occasional impatient drumming of my fingers on
the steering wheel.

As we approached the slip road from the roundabout I
moved through the gears and broke ranks, 'Look, will you
stop that ...'

He bit, 'Stop what?'

'Lying there like Lenin on his catafalque, frozen in
gloom.'

He huffed loudly. 'You've no idea, have you?'

I turned to catch a glimpse of him with his gaping mouth
animating his look only slightly. 'No idea of what?'

'What you've done ... going in there and noising up
Grantie. He's not a man to be messed with.'

I couldn't believe what I was hearing. This, from the
man who had just about twisted my arm from its socket to
get me to help Grantie. And the same man who had done
his level best to allay my fears about working with a group
that gave me the dry boak.

'Andy, am I hearing you right?' I flicked on the blinkers, pulled into a bus stop.

'You'll have no trouble hearing Grantie if he gets going, that's for sure.'

I stopped the car. 'He doesn't scare me, mate ... I've met uglier than Davie Grant.'

'You haven't seen him angry, yet ...'

I remembered something my father told me, it must have been when I was in Primary 7, no later: *If you lose your temper, you lose the argument.* Grown men didn't gain advantage throwing their weight around; it was the opposite. The adult world was all about keeping it in and flattering to deceive. Very few got to operate outside of those boundaries though, I conceded, perhaps Davie Grant was one of them.

'And you're telling me this now, Andy?' My inference was clear.

'Look, you're getting a good drink out of this, why can't you just play the game?'

I held my breath for a moment, made sure my heart settled, said, 'Is that what this lad's death is to him – a game? Is that what you think it is, Andy? Because it's not that for me. Not by a long stretch. Death by murder is not something I can make light of; it's not in my make-up.'

Andy turned away, shook his head. An old man with a bunnet and hospital-issue walking stick made for the bus shelter. Andy let him pass the car before he replied.

'I'm not trying to trivialise Stevie's death, just the opposite. This is a serious business to Grantie, I can tell that, I know that! If I'd known you were going to jump in and have a go at him, I'd never have suggested you get involved.' Andy's mouth tightened like a snare. All at once his posture changed, it was as if he'd caught himself out.

'What do you mean *suggested* ... you suggested me to Grantie?'

Andy touched his mouth, pressed the underside of his palm into the gape then jerked his hand onto the dash with a slap. 'Look, Doug, it's complicated, all right?'

'Not too complicated, I hope, Andy. Because my backside's on the line here.'

'Yours and mine, mate!'

A bus pulled up behind us, its sign said it was heading for the top of the town. The old fella with the stick started to hirple his way towards the doors.

Andy made to get out. 'I'm going to grab the bus, I'll give you a bell later.'

'Andy ... I'll drop you off.'

'No thanks,' he put a black look on me, 'you've done quite enough for me today.' He slammed the door and jogged for the bus. I watched the driver admonishing me for parking in front of the stop sign, hands waving over the giant wheel, and started to pull out.

I drove for the Loaning and headed home, I knew Lyn would be there. We had things to say, about the house and whether or not I could actually bring myself to sell. About the future and making something of the rapidly diminishing time we had left. The situation stung me: I was messing with her dreams now, too.

Lyn was sitting in the kitchen with a mug of coffee and a copy of the *Radio Times* when I got home. She looked so settled, domesticated, that it hit me between the eyes.

'You're back early,' she put down the magazine, rose to place a peck on my cheek.

'Yeah, well, it wasn't the most productive of days.'

'Really. Well, I probably shouldn't ask.' She returned to the kettle and flicked the switch, was spooning coffee into another cup when she spoke again. 'I don't think the day's a total write-off, mind you.'

'And why's that?'

The kettle started to make a noise like a puncture in a tyre. 'Do you remember that picture you took on your phone, the one I got you to send to me?'

'To show to Glenn ... yeah, of course I remember.'

'Well, he finally got back to me and he told me something I think you'll find very interesting.'

'Go on ...'

'That boy's a well-known drug dealer, in fact he's the town's go-to guy for disco biscuits.'

I stored the information away for processing at a later date. 'He's sure about this?'

'Oh aye ... and even more interestingly, that Jan Milne lassie he was with has a bit of a rep herself, she's one of the crowd's groupies.'

'Did Glenn say anything about Steven Nichols?'

Lyn started to pour the water over the coffee granules. 'No, sorry ... Stevie's a bit of a mystery to him.'

I took the cup off the counter, my hopes of a break evaporating. 'Me too, more's the pity.'

Chapter 30

I spent a restless night, steeped in dreams that looked like the director's cut of *Dark City*. A little guy in a black-leather trench coat, with a bald head and a set of features he'd taken from my friend Andy, was following me around. There was no Shell Beach, not even an Ayr Beach, but I knew the landscape only too well. The black haunts of my imagination, the hollows of my subconscious, where my waking fears chased shadows into the unknown tomb of my soul.

I sat on the edge of the bed rubbing the stubble on my chin, it felt like an industrial belt-grinder. My head hurt too, seemed to hurt inside and out, as though even the faculty of thought created pain. I touched my temples, tried to inveigh some sense of soothing, but nothing seemed to halt the onslaught. I sensed it was there for the day.

I twisted my neck, turned to see Lyn in heavy sleep, her arms spread above the duvet, her fingers clawing at an imaginary keyboard. I wondered what went on with her, in her mind. And then a scowl crossed her face, she seemed to be dreaming, or maybe it was me – still in a hypnopompic state that was looking more like my real world every day.

I took my clothes and shoes into the bathroom and dressed quietly; I didn't want to wake Lyn because, truth told, I was in no mood for chat.

Even in the height of a Scottish summer the water in the pipes of the old home was cold as I splashed my face and neck: it felt good, calming, reassuring somehow. A good dunking in cold water seemed to me like just what my head ordered. I was out of blades, and my growth too long for the electric razor, so the stubbled look would have to be *in* again, at least for today. I nearly laughed at the thought of myself as a trend setter. As I pulled on my T-shirt and black, greying cords and clocked my image in the mirror I looked like the 'before' picture from a GQ magazine make-over.

'Rough isn't in it, Doug ...'

The kitchen was cold and desolate; the lack of a greeting from Ben, tail wagging and tongue lolling, still cut deep. I had no notion to eat, or take coffee even. I wanted out. Away.

I searched the cupboard where I'd started to keep the collection of pills, potions and unguents that the over-40s needed on an almost daily basis. My stomach was churning and my head still sore, I felt like I was battling a hangover, but there had been no drink the night before.

The Andrew's Salts foamed away as I popped some Anadin from the pack. There had been a time when an early morning heart-starter would have got me going, but those days were long gone. I'd promised myself I wasn't going to become like the old timers on the force – slamming whisky and Gaviscon because their guts were too tender to take the hard stuff on its own. It made me think of Andy again; more and more he was becoming the bellwether of what I could have become. I hoped this latest run-in with Davie Grant hadn't sent him scurrying to the bottle.

I checked on Lyn again, she was still sleeping. It seemed best to leave her, I certainly wasn't about to wake her to say I was going out. She could suss that for herself and I needed her to figure out that sometimes I just had to be alone.

And now was one of those times. I took the car up the drive, headed for the Carrick hills. The Audi almost spat out the low-gears, it wanted to feel the engine's burn, so I opened the throttle. The tyres hadn't warmed to the road, spun a little, then started to screech. I had barely hit fourth before Doonfoot was a mere pinpoint in my rear-view mirror.

I headed over the hills, out past Maidens and on through the wind of green fields and tight turns. This was my place to think, to clear my head. I came here when there was something bothering me, but there were so many things bothering me now they competed for my attention.

I couldn't get my head around the house sale issue and I certainly couldn't bring myself to make it a priority when I had the case to solve. Steven Nichols' death had gone from being a point of interest to a plain sore point. It seemed even discussing the facts with Andy tightened the tension between us.

'What the hell is his problem?' I blurted out to no one.

I knew fine well what the answer was – he was keeping something from me – and I knew I'd need to raise it with Andy soon. I had my suspicions about what it might be, but then I'd been wrong before, and hoped I was this time.

I took the Audi into a tight bend, dropped speed and then tanned it on the straight again. I made the approach into Maybole at the top of the road's limit then put the anchors on; the by-pass was only a few short streets away.

'Okay, time for answers.'

I made a mental route through Maybole, down the by-pass, and on to Prestwick.

Davie Grant's reaction to the news that I'd found out he was once in the frame for the Nichols murder was not unexpected. He was a hot-head, my only surprise that his reaction wasn't more volcanic. And Andy would come round – he was an old friend. It was the information from Lyn's son about Jan Milne and her boyfriend that had really troubled my sleep.

'The drugs don't work …' I spoke from experience; booze and fast-powders only brought more demons to the party. But what was the link between Jan's new druggie boyfriend and the death of her last one?

I knew I was, at best, clutching at straws. Was there even a link to find? I didn't know the answer to that question, but I knew if it was a 'no' then I was facing complete darkness. Sometimes an investigation was about following leads, sometimes it was about following your gut and sometimes it was about attaching the tenuous threads of the two together and making a wish.

As I pulled onto Prestwick Main Street the traffic suddenly changed from slow to going nowhere.

'Come on, come on …' The commuter routes clogged up earlier every day, it seemed. I checked the clock on the dash, there was still plenty of time to catch Bert Nichols and hear what he had to say for himself about the most recent turn of events.

Chapter 31

I parked round the back of Flannagan's and took the side-lane that skirted the police station and the taxi rank. The main drag was still gridlocked as I shimmied through the traffic, cars filled with faces dour as 'get oot!' on the way to work. Even with their doleful eyes following me, envious of my ability to move freely about town with no desk-shackles calling me, I still felt a twinge of regret that I wasn't among their number.

The force had been my life for so long that so many of the old ways were impossible to shake. I didn't miss the bleary-eyed early mornings, where the first coffee of the day barely cancelled out the taste of toothpaste, or the repetitive grind of the day-in, day-out. But I missed the real reason I was there: to give my life meaning.

Somewhere along the way I let the job get under my skin, change me. There were blokes who saw it as no more than a job at the best of times but there were the ones – who I gravitated to – that understood why we were there. People were savages, no more, no less. If you gave them the chance they reverted to form and ran wild. They needed consequences to control their actions and that's where we came in.

I liked to think of the force as the last civilising line

we had but I know at times it had the potential to turn its strongest adherents into just what they despised the most. Take away the triumphs and the warm glow that duty delivered and every day was a test of how hard you held the reins of humanity. Someone once said, 'The price of life is eternal vigilance'. That's exactly how it felt on the force. For me, anyway.

Bert Nichols' home was a neat sandstone bungalow on Caerlaverock Avenue. He opened the door as the chimes of the bell were still ringing. As he stood in the hallway he laced a navy tie through the white collars of his shirt.

'Mr Michie ... I wasn't expecting you.'

'Can I come in?'

He nodded. 'Of course.'

We seemed to have the house to ourselves; it was excruciatingly prim and tidy, the place probably made dust too nervous to settle. I took a chintzy chair in the front room and waved away the offer of tea. As I sat facing the straight-backed Bert, I stared at the white patch of cloth resting on the chair behind him. I wondered if the patch of cloth had ever had contact with the back of a head? It seemed unlikely, the artefact was as starched as Papal vestments; the irony of the image in my head wasn't lost to me when I realised who I was staring at.

'Well, to what do I owe the pleasure?' Bert was nonplussed to see me in his home at silly-o'clock in the morning.

I chose my reply carefully. 'I followed your advice and spoke to DI John Scott.'

He arched an eyebrow but remained silent.

'Yes, he led my investigation up some very interesting avenues.'

'He did?'

'I think you must have known he would, Bert ... why

else would you give me that tip at the Fourways, unless you wanted to put Davie Grant back in the frame for your son's murder?'

I expected my remark to have the same effect as detonating a hand grenade in the room, but Bert kept his impassive stare. If he had a grudge against Grant, he hid it well.

'That's not why I made the suggestion.'

'Then why?'

Bert removed the face of his watch from beneath his shirtsleeve. 'What else has your investigation turned up so far, Mr Michie?'

It wasn't a brusque dismissal of my question, I could tell he intended to be frank with me, perhaps once he was sure we were singing from the same hymn sheet.

'Some very interesting facts about your son's girlfriend ... and the company she's been keeping.'

Bert nibbled at his lower lip, rose from the chair. As he walked to the broad bay window he put his hands behind his back and laced fingers in a contorted knot.

'We didn't ... approve of the girl.'

'Jan Milne?'

The sound of her name sent Bert twisting back to face me. 'That's her, yes.'

'And why would that be?' I knew the answer to the question but I wanted to hear it from him.

Bert's voice rose an octave. 'Look, if you've checked her out, I think you'll know why.'

'She says you and your wife didn't like her.'

'She has some very louche ways ... and associates.'

'Did you feel she was leading Steven astray?'

He unclasped his hands. 'I honestly don't know who was leading who, Mr Michie.' Bert returned to his seat but continued to stare towards the broad window at the front of the room. His demeanour seemed to have altered, it was almost imperceptible in someone so buttoned-up but there was now a calm, resigned look about him. It felt like the time to press him for an answer to my earlier question.

'Bert, why did you ask me to seek out DI Scott?'

'You don't know ... I mean, it's not obvious to you?'

I shook my head.

Bert gazed at me with watery eyes, 'Scott's drugs squad, I mean, that's his bread and butter, anyway. I thought you'd know that, given your line of work and the fact that this town's half-full of drug addicts.'

The remark caught me off guard, sent my mind carving out new neural paths.

'Are you saying your son was involved in drugs?'

'No. I'm not saying that.'

'Then what are you saying, Bert?'

He stood up and headed for the door, a new look of impatience building. 'I need to get to work,' he grabbed the handle and indicated the hallway carpet, 'so if you don't mind ...'

Chapter 32

I wandered out of Bert Nichols' house in a daze. There seemed to be so much going on beneath the surface that I couldn't keep my feet on solid ground anymore. Nothing made sense, and I knew when that was the case it was because people were concealing the truth.

I'd reached the Red Lion in a daze, I was back on the main drag, before I dragged myself into the real world once again. I took a deep breath, found I was glancing backwards for no apparent reason, and then I caught sight of Bert's car heading out of town.

He seemed stolid, a fine upright citizen, but I knew there was more to him than met the eye. I could almost excuse his dalliance with the Order as an anachronism of his generation, an old-school brainwashing that had once been rife in the west-coast of Scotland. Who knows how the Order first got their hooks into him? Grantie was a meat-head, a bigot and the crass kind of bully that predominated in Ayrshire. I could see the appeal for him, his type liked the trappings of seeming importance, the feeling of being big time, the crowd at their back.

I started to cross the road, walk against the traffic, until I reached the other side. I was merely a few hundred yards from Jan Milne's flat – the one she had once shared with

Steven Nichols. I told myself it was time I rattled her cage once again.

As I stood outside the door to the communal staircase I heard the sound of heels clacking on stone steps. I dived to the side of the door, out of view of the window, and waited for someone to appear. A broad woman in her bad-fifties emerged, panting with exertion and almost bounding for the pavement. I slipped my arm in the rapidly closing gap and eased myself in the doorway.

At Jan Milne's flat I put my ear to the door, there was a radio blaring out the WestSound jingle. I knocked and stepped back. For a moment the volume decreased, I knocked again.

As the front door started to open I made sure my foot was in position to hold it there.

'Hello, Jan ...'

'You!'

I forced my way in. 'No other ...'

'Hey, what are you doing?'

I walked into the living room and waited for her to follow. She appeared as if on cue.

'Sorry about that, Jan, I'm not normally so heavy handed but I didn't think you'd lay on the good biccies for me.'

'I want you to leave.'

I shrugged off her suggestion, then lowered myself into the comfortable sofa. 'It really is a very nice place you have here.'

She folded her arms in front of me and looked over the bridge of her nose. 'What the hell do you want?'

'I thought we could pick up from where we left off the last time ... you remember, before your new boyfriend with the flashy motor cut in.'

'He's not my boyfriend.'

'Oh, no?' I crossed my legs, tried to look nonchalant. 'I

heard he was. I know he's just your type anyway, flash with the cash and a man who's connected to the big scores.'

She shook her head. 'You've got me all wrong.'

'Is that right? Well, maybe you should set the record straight ... come and sit down, Jan.'

She turned towards the door we had just come through, looked pensively at the distance. Did she consider bolting? If she did, she thought better of it, sat herself down in front of me and looked at her fingernails.

'I don't know what you want from me.'

I firmed my voice. 'I'm investigating a murder, show some sense girl.'

She curled her red fingernails into her palms to make fists. 'I can't help you.'

'Can't or won't?'

She rolled her eyes, then scrunched them tight. Two China-blue lids clamped themselves over her gaze.

I spoke. 'You said Steven's parents were controlling ... what did you mean by that?'

'Strict, y'know, they were his parents and didn't much like the company he kept.'

'Including you?'

Her eyes came into view again. 'Yes. Including me.'

'Now why would that be, a lovely girl like you?'

'I don't know. You'd have to ask them. I don't know what goes on in other peoples' heads.'

I sat forward in the chair and fixed a serious stare on her. 'Oh, I have Jan. I've asked a lot of people about you. Do you know what they say? They say you're a very particular kind of girl. A stop-out. A bad-lad groupie ...'

She didn't deny it, just broke our gaze and looked over to the other side of the room.

'Your new man's a dealer, but I bet you know that.'

She never flinched, just kept her eyes front.

'What was it that first attracted you to Stevie?'

She pinched her nose. 'What?'

'Steven Nichols ... your late ex, remember him?'

Jan crouched over, dug her elbows on her thighs and buried her face in her hands. 'Why are you doing this?'

I rose, bellowed at her: 'Because a boy was murdered and you can point the finger.'

'I can't!'

'Yes you can ... now tell me why? Was it because Stevie was into drugs, too? Did he run up a debt with someone? Is that it?'

'No ...' she screamed, tears coming full and fast now.

'The flash lad with the car, did Stevie owe him? Is that what you're doing with him now, working off Stevie's debt on your back?'

She lunged for me with her nails out, 'Shut your mouth, just shut it!'

I grabbed her arms, shook her. She screamed at me, more tears flowed. 'I know all about Davie Grant and I know all about DI Scott – is that why you're afraid to speak to me? Are you frightened I'll find out about your involvement in this mess?'

'No. Leave me ...'

'Jan, you need me, I'm your only friend in all of this. You know you're messing with serious people. If they can do away with Stevie, what's to stop them coming for you next?'

'You don't know what you're talking about, Grantie was Stevie's friend ... he was always saying what he was going to do for, Stevie. They had big plans together. Grantie wouldn't hurt him.' She went limp in my arms, started to cry harder, deep heavy sobs from the core of her.

I let her down on the couch, she curled up and looked like a small child. I felt a twinge of guilt for pushing her so far, I saw now that she didn't have any more to give me. She believed she had given me nothing, that she'd protected her friends, her group, but what she'd actually done was firm a suspicion that had been building in my mind.

I closed the door gently on my way out.

Chapter 33

I collected the Audi from the back of Flannagan's and headed home. At the King Street roundabout I watched two junkies in a kerfuffle, prodding each other and lunging to grab hair. It looked like a Saturday night drunks' squabble slowed down to a third of the normal speed. No one at the cop shop over the road seemed even slightly interested in the goings; you start locking up junkies for street brawls, where does it stop? Even if you packed them in like sardines there weren't enough cells in the place.

I ploughed on through the wreckage of the Sandgate, the scaffolding over those scabby buildings at the bridge fooling nobody. They were like the Forth Bridge – needed painting round the clock – a lick of emulsion once in a blue moon wasn't going to cut it. I felt a turn in my gut at the thought of the now moribund town; I wanted out more than anything because I couldn't stand back and watch the place decay like it was doing.

By Belmont, at the tip of the level-crossing, I caught a WestSound news bulletin, nothing stood out except the news that some of the pubs were finding trading so tough they were going down to three-day weeks.

'A recipe for disaster, that,' I blasted the radio.

The hard-core would double their intake on the three

days, make the weekend a long weekend – and it would be very long for the police troops in attendance. A stark image of the Auld Toun's slow descent into purgatory burned itself on my mind. I'd seen what the atrophy had done to the likes of Andy, medicated on booze to make it bearable, and I didn't relish the prospect for myself.

The sky was a low grey wash over the rooftops of Alloway as I pulled into the drive at my old family home. There was still some warmth in the air, a hint to the summer just passed, but we were now a long way from the familiar aromas of freshly-cut grass and barbecue steaks grilling. I felt a pressure of ebbing time set itself up in my chest.

Lyn was heading for the kitchen as I opened the front door and stepped inside.

'Oh, hello ...'

I nodded. 'Hi.'

She stopped in her tracks, turned. 'You look like it's been a hard day at the office.'

A smirk. 'You could say that.'

She seemed to intuit my mood matched my expression. 'Grab a seat, I'll get you a coffee.'

'That would be fabulous, thank you.'

I slumped in the living room, the place seemed colder than I remembered it of late. Not much, merely a few degrees. But perceptible.

Lyn handed over the coffee mug. 'Come on, then, out with it.'

'What?'

'You've a face like a stopped clock.'

'Oh, that ...'

'Yes, that. Is it the case?'

I nodded. 'It's just playing on my mind, that's all.'

Lyn sipped her coffee. 'Well, a problem shared and all that.'

'I don't want to burden you. You've enough on your plate.'

She tilted her head towards her shoulder, 'Burden me, *please ...*'

I figured that giving voice to some of my concerns might actually help. Lyn had a sharp mind, if there were any connections I'd missed she'd point them out to me. There was also the fact that she was a woman and a mother – with an altogether different perspective on things.

I filled Lyn in on the latest developments in the investigation: on Davie Grant's status as a suspect; on Bert's uptight reaction this morning and on Jan Milne's insistence that Grantie and Steven Nichols were nothing short of bestos.

Lyn held her cup like she was drawing warmth from it. As she spoke, her words were a curious drawl I hadn't observed before. 'There's something very odd about the way Bert treated his son ... I mean, when they get to a certain age you have to let them make their own mistakes or they won't grow into adults.'

'Jan said the Nichols kept Stevie on a short leash.'

'Well that sounds like a classic recipe for rebellion, if you ask me.'

I had to agree, even though I had nothing to back up the assumption. 'That could be why he was with Jan?'

'Yeah, she sounds the ultimate bad girl to get their backs up.' Her coffee was finished, she lowered the mug onto the carpet. 'Do you think Stevie was involved with drugs?'

'It's the logical conclusion ... Bert Nichols has inferred Grantie's up to his neck in drugs and Stevie worked for him.'

'That doesn't mean much.'

'Well, Jan said Stevie and Grantie were full of plans. Sounded like Grantie had a fast-track mapped out for the boy.'

'Maybe it wasn't fast enough.'

I caught onto her reasoning immediately. 'You mean, Stevie got overly-ambitious and bit off more than he could chew.'

Lyn shrugged. 'Maybe he wanted a bigger share of the action.'

If Steven Nichols was the type to fall in with the wrong crowd – be it because he wanted to sever the apron strings or not – he was certainly going to be the type to get big ideas about himself. I'd known more than a few dealers who ended up in the ground because of their hubris.

'Yeah, it's an option ... but then so is the exact opposite.'

'You mean Stevie pulled back from Grantie's offer. But what if it was an offer he couldn't refuse?'

I tipped my head back onto the sofa and sighed out. 'This is my problem, it's all speculation.'

Lyn rose, collected up the coffee cups. 'Fancy another?'

I nodded. 'Why not.'

Through long years of brain melting detective work I'd learned when to turn the whole puzzle over to my subconscious. Batting things about in the front of the mind for too long rarely delivers answers; rarely delivers anything other than a headache, to be truthful. I sank deeper into the sofa and resolved to put the case out of my thoughts for a little while.

Lyn returned with two refills. 'Well, any further forward?'

'Not really,' I said. 'There's only one certainty at this point in time ...'

'What's that?'

'Whatever Steven Nichols' involvement in the drugs trade, his father wouldn't have liked it.'

'I'd say Bert would be near Pentecostal in that regard.'

I raised my mug again, 'You're right ... and I'd say that'd cause quite a rift in the Order.'

Chapter 34

It doesn't matter how much time you spend in big cities, after a short while you become inured to their excesses. In Belfast I turned a wry eye to the legions of shoddy street performers that flocked in the summer months, chasing the tourist shilling. Edinburgh was the same, at festival time you didn't want to be navigating the Royal Mile at any hour. But you cut the cities some slack for the fact that they were able to absorb the changes; cities were big enough to be mutable, places like the Auld Toun were not.

I don't know whether it was because Ayr was so far removed from city status that it shocked me to see junkies crashed out in shop doorways or whether it was because I'd seen nothing like it in all my years of association with the place. 'I've called the police,' a dislocated voice boomed in my general direction.

'Y'what?'

'The police ...' It was a woman in a Greggs' pinafore, she pointed to the shop front where a pile of amorphous clothing and bony joints lay huddled in a pool of urine.

'Wouldn't you be better calling an ambulance?' I said.

A tut. Loud one.

'That'll be right, I don't want to be accused of prolonging another sorry existence like that.' She stood over the ragged near-corpse of the junkie and pulled a girn that the late Les Dawson would have been proud of. As the flashing lights and sirens appeared I headed off down the High Street, assured in the knowledge I wasn't the only one whose love affair with the Auld Toun had turned sour.

In Bridge's pub I nodded to the regulars and scanned the length of the bar for Andy. The place was quiet, only a few dole moles and a crusty old bluenose clamped onto the sports pages of the *Daily Record*.

The barman appeared, polishing a glass with a white towel. 'What can I get you?'

I wasn't there for a drink, I was there to find my friend. 'No sign of Andy?'

He removed the towel from the glass, stationed it with the other pint mugs on a shelf below the bar. 'Just what you see here, mate.'

I didn't know what to think; Bridge's without Andy at this hour was like New York abandoning the Sinatra soundtrack.

I felt a tug on my coat sleeve. 'He's drinking in O'Brien's now.'

I turned, clocked an old fella with sad drinker's eyes, a road-map of burst blood vessels running the gamut of nose and cheeks. 'O'Brien's, that's a bit of a schlep up there.'

The old boy shrugged. 'Bumped into him at Fish Cross earlier, says he's after a change.'

It didn't sound like the Andy I knew. He wasn't big on changes; was still wearing Adidas Samba for crying out loud.

I left Bridge's and crossed the Sandgate, followed it all the way to Barns Street and then onto the top of the town. As I passed the Ayrshire & Galloway I thought O'Brien's seemed like a strange choice of drinker for Andy to pick, unless he was trying to go under the radar – which was quite likely.

The bar was quiet, more staff than customers at this hour. Situated across from the train station it picked up the odd day-tripper and those waiting for a return to Glasgow, but had nothing that you'd call a regular crowd.

I spotted Andy huddled in the corner of the snug with a pint of heavy.

'You're a long way from Kansas ...'

He looked up, frowned. Dropped his gloomy eyes back to the pint. That's when I noticed the shiner – a brutal black gouge to the side of his left eye that looked to have been delivered with some precision.

'Been in the wars?'

He looked away, 'You should see the other guy.'

'I bet he gave his knuckles a bad scrape.'

Andy picked up his pint, drained a good third in one pelt. When he released the glass from his lips, his demeanour seemed to have changed, like he was too tired to maintain the charade.

'How did you find me?'

'Your answering service in Bridge's.' I sat down in front of him. 'What's going on?'

'His eyes widened. 'What do you mean?'

'I mean the obvious ... your eye, the change of second residence.'

His gaze fell gloomily into the dark pint. 'Nothing ...'

'Do I look like I'm buying that?' I reached out and pressed the underside of his chin. 'That's a serious working over.'

He winced, shot a hand to the side of his torso.

'Ribs sore too?'

'Look, you're a bit late to the party, if that's your plan.'

'Meaning?'

'*Meaning*, Doug, the damage is done and if you're half the friend you claim to be then you'll pull your neck in.'

He didn't seem to be referring to the wind-up. 'What do you mean?'

'I mean, Doug, your little stint with Grantie the other day had some repercussions. The case is closed, you might say.'

My mind swam. I knew Grantie was a low-life, a tin-pot hard man, but I didn't think he had it in him to mess with someone's features. Certainly not over a bit of word jousting.

'Grantie did this to you?'

'No. Grantie doesn't like getting out of breath. That's why he has a payroll.'

The inference was clear, it was supposed to be some kind of message for me. My nerves shrieked when I thought of Lyn at home, alone.

'God ... Lyn.'

'What about her?'

'She's back at my folks' house, on her own.' I got out of my chair, 'Come on, you're coming with me.'

He pulled his arm from my grasp. 'What? No chance.'

'Listen, *mate*, you got me into this and unless you want to make that a pair of shiners, I'd get your backside moving pretty sharpish.'

Andy shuffled around the table; briefly clasping his pint as he went, he managed a couple of slugs before placing the glass on the shelf by the door.

Chapter 35

In the harsh daylight I saw that Andy's face had been battered worse than I first thought, the dim lighting of O'Brien's obviously hiding the worst of his injuries. He coughed and wheezed as he went, clamping a hand on his ribcage and grimacing widely. He looked like a man near the end of the road; he didn't know how close he was, but if anything had happened to Lyn I'd make sure he found out.

'I can't believe what you've got me into, Andy.'

He struggled for breath, words fell between gasps. 'Look, don't go pointing the finger at me ... it was you that rattled Grantie's cage. I told you not to noise him up.'

I put hard eyes on Andy. He had done all but beg me to take this case and now that it had turned nasty he was backtracking. 'A favour, you said ... please Doug, for me, you said.'

He halted in the street outside Rabbie's. 'You were supposed just take a look, put his mind at rest ... you weren't supposed to go this far.'

I grabbed Andy's collar. 'I'll go a lot further now.'

He pushed me away. 'No. It's over ... the case is closed as far as Grantie's concerned.' He dug in his pocket and produced a white envelope. 'Here's your wages in full. Now let it be.'

I had an urge to laugh in his face but the brief feeling passed quickly. 'Over? Not a chance. This case is closed when I say so.' I stepped up to Andy's chest and tipped some steel in my voice. 'And you're going to see it through with me.'

I marched towards the car, tugging Andy behind me as I went. He kept his mouth shut, but I could tell he was rattled. It wasn't so much the threat of my continuing the investigation, but the real and present threat that Grantie had obviously put on him.

I wanted to know just what it was that Davie Grant held over my friend, but the time wasn't right to ask that. There had to be some hook that he had in him, but I didn't know what it might be. I saw now that Andy had changed, his behaviour had altered dramatically from when I last knew him. I had put it down to time, the passing of the years and the fact that we'd both went off in opposite directions for so long. But I saw now that he had turned into something I didn't like. There was a desperation in him; perhaps it had always been there and I'd translated it as a need, an ambition to get on, get ahead, but when that went it had been supplanted with a different urge altogether.

On the road out to Alloway I kept checking the rear-view for signs of us being followed, or prowling police cars. The steering wheel grew hot in my palms but it was nothing compared to the heat building inside my head and the fears I had for Lyn, alone in that house with no one to protect her. If any hurt befell her I'd never forgive myself, or Andy.

'Tell me what it is he has over you, Andy.' I let the words fall like incendiary devices, I wasn't taking any more double-talk from him.

'What are you on about?'

'Grantie ... you didn't just bump into him on some piping job at the Lodge.' The idea seemed ridiculous in light of recent events. 'I'm on about your face, or more particularly the cuts and bruises. He didn't serve those up as a thank you.'

'That was a disagreement.'

I spat at him, 'Disagreement, pull the other one!'

Andy sank into the seat, fiddled with the window and tried to inveigle some breeze to cool himself down.

'I told you, you overstepped the mark with him. He doesn't like that sort of thing.'

I threw the car into the hairpin bend at the top of Laughlanglen, 'Am I missing something? Like, when did you start taking a good slapping as a matter of course?'

'There's one of me and hundreds of them, I'm hardly in a position to fight back.'

'Why's he hard-arming you, Andy? What does he have on you?'

'Nothing ...'

'I don't believe you. You wouldn't have got me, and now Lyn, mixed up in all of this if he didn't have a pretty big stick to beat you with.'

Andy fell quiet as we pulled into the driveway, it was as if I'd timed his escape clause perfectly. I flung open the car door and ran to the house.

Inside, I yelled out, 'Lyn ... Lyn ...'

I heard Andy running from the car. 'No sign of her?'

I stamped through to the kitchen, it was empty. 'Lyn ...'

Andy followed, yelling. We paced the house, upstairs and down.

'Where is she?' I said, my voice rasping now with all the shouting.

'Lyn ... can you hear us?' yelled Andy.

There was no sign of her. I felt an almighty hurt unfolding in my chest, it spread to my shoulders and froze in my neck. I felt tense, sick. I drew fists and fought the urge to vomit where I stood. 'Oh, God, no ...'

Andy laid a hand on my arm. 'Doug, I'm sorry.'

'You're sorry.'

'I only ...'

'You only what? Thought of yourself.'

'No, Doug.'

I yelled at him. 'Just shut up, would you. Can't you see you've done enough damage. Who knows where she is now, or what that nut-job's done to her.'

'I don't know what to say. I'm in your hands, Doug. I'm sorry.'

'Start with the truth ... what does he have on you, Andy?'

His head fell to his chest, a few stumbled words came on the back of a sigh. 'Money. I owe him ... not much, well, it wasn't much.'

'Money for what? You live like a pauper.'

'I had some troubles with the drink and I got reckless, gambling and ... look, does it matter?'

'Does it matter?' I pushed him aside. 'God, does anything, Andy? Does it matter to you that Lyn's missing?'

I walked downstairs, Andy trailed behind me. As I picked up the telephone receiver he spoke.

'Who are you calling?'

'Who do you think? The police.'

'Doug, now come on, think about what you're doing.' He moved in front of me, tried to take the phone from my hand.

'Leave it, Andy ... you've done quite enough.'

Chapter 36

The ringing phone was answered quickly.

'Hello, DI Scott.'

'It's Doug Michie.'

I watched Andy walk to the front of the room and grab a fistful of hair. He had no true concept of the trouble he'd caused.

I spoke into the receiver. 'I'd like to meet up with you, soon as possible.'

His tone changed. 'I thought we'd said all we had to say to each other.'

'Not by far ...'

'And what's that supposed to mean?'

'Do you want to take the risk of discussing this on the phone or do you want to meet me?'

There was a pause on the line. If he was thinking, DI Scott was taking his time about it. 'I'm not sure I like being at your beck and call, Mr Michie.'

'It's more a matter of *quid pro quo* ... If you help me out, I'm pretty sure I can help you out.'

The pause was shorter this time. 'Meet me at the Auld Kirk.'

'Half an hour.'

I hung up.

Andy was still staring through the window at the garden, the back of his head a looming invitation for me to rabbit-punch. I resisted, turned for the door, and then heard the sound of water rushing through the pipes upstairs. The next sound was a lock turning. As the bathroom door slid open, Lyn appeared with a towel wrapped around her. Long dark tendrils whipped at her shoulders as she stepped back in shock.

'When did you get back?' she yelled.

I looked up, speechless. Andy appeared behind me. We watched together as Lyn removed the tiny ear-phones of her iPod Shuffle from beneath her damp hair. 'What are you pair up to? Standing there, ogling me ...'

Andy's face broke into a wide smile. 'Don't ask ... we're just very glad to see you!'

She tightened the towel round herself, 'Perverts!'

The steps seemed steeper than usual as I pounded up them to grab Lyn. She looked at me like I'd lost my marbles. It was on my lips to tell her how I thought we'd lost her, how things had taken a dramatic turn for the worse, but I let it slide as I watched her trail off to the bedroom.

'I'm going out, Lyn. I'll leave Andy to keep you company.'

Andy trudged through to the front room. I headed for the door but stuck my head in the living room as I went. 'You keep an eye on her, do you hear me?'

'I don't think she's the one I need to keep an eye on ... Sure you don't want me to come with you?'

The idea that Andy, with his bruised ribs and shiner, was going to be any help was laughable. 'I think I'll manage ... don't let Lyn out of your sight, though.'

I headed for the car.

The pot-holed and scarred roads of Alloway tested the suspension, even on the sports model. If this was supposed to be the premier part of Ayr, I dreaded to think how places like Jabba had fared lately.

I passed the white-washed stone of Burns' Cottage, made it through a hubcap-sized roundabout onto Monument Road and headed for the auld haunted kirk.

'Whare ghaists and houlets nightly cry.'

DI John Scott was already in place, his car parked on the opposite side of the wide street, his burly frame standing sentry at the kirk gates. As I pulled up I saw him start to head for the kirkyard. He was standing over a flat headstone as I arrived on the scene.

'So, why are we here, Mr Michie?'

It was undoubtedly a question I had no simple answer to. The truthful answer was close to an admission that I was on a fishing expedition, of sorts. The optimistic answer, however, was that with some blurring of the lines of official police procedure, we could help each other out. I opted for a strategy of laying all my cards on the table at once.

I told DI Scott what I'd uncovered about the death of Steven Nichols. I made the details about the drugs trade sound greater than they were, to gauge his reaction, but he did little more than shift his gaze from the middle distance. The definite connections I'd found between Davie Grant and Stevie had more of an impact, but my overall impression was that the DI was unimpressed.

'I don't know how far back the animosity between Bert and Grantie runs, but there's definite conflict there,' I said.

'It goes way back, trust me,' said the DI. 'Some of it's vintage, too.'

'Stevie had some very divided loyalties to contend with ... the entire scene's a cesspit of warped ideas. It's no wonder the boy took a knife, I'd say they've been flying about for a good while.'

DI Scott took out a cigarette, sparked up. He looked contemplative as he turned the conversation back on itself.

'Look, this is all very interesting, Doug ... but it's conjecture. There's no facts, what do you expect me to do?'

I wanted him to add to my theories, one in particular. 'There's a power play in the Order. I think Bert and Grantie were split over the drugs scene – there's no way Bert would be for that – when he found out his son was up to his neck in it, heads had to roll. Stevie just got caught in the crossfire.'

DI Scott drew deep on his cig. 'Prove it.'

'I can't.'

The face behind the dark beard sat granite firm. 'I *know* you can't.'

It was time to drop the hammer. If Scott was as good a detective as I thought he was, then he had the missing pieces of the puzzle that I needed. I just had to convince him to share them.

'You know, it's Ulster that pulls the Order's strings. I built my career there, I know the place. I know there's a fear, a downright nervousness, of Scottish independence in some quarters. Tempers are fraught at the idea of the rest of the union falling like dominos.'

The more I spoke about Ulster, the greater attention I seemed to glean from Scott. 'What are you saying, Michie?'

'The power struggle between Bert and Grantie's just window dressing – the bigger picture's about the Order augmenting, going up the gears – if you tell me who's pulling the levers in Ulster, then we can find out who killed Stevie Nichols.'

DI Scott dropped his cigarette on the paving flags, stamped it out. 'What makes you think I'm interested?'

'You don't care about the death of one little Orange boyo, but you have bigger sharks to fry – like the one turning your patch into Zombieland.'

The idea of collaring a bigger player in the drugs trade appealed to the DI. 'Supposing you're right, what guarantee do I have that there's anything in it for me?'

He started to walk out of the kirkyard.

I called him back. 'John, you underestimate how deep my roots are spread in Ulster. You give me the name of the Order's contact and I'll deliver you the drugs source – there's not a scrote I can't dig out there, all I need's a name.'

He turned on his heels, smirked. 'I've never found the RUC to be in the slightest bit helpful in the past.'

'That's where you've been going wrong. You see I'm not RUC, anymore.'

Chapter 37

DI John Scott gave up the name of the Order's contact in Ulster. I knew it wasn't through any sense of decency, or misplaced altruism. Scott couldn't care less about the death of Stevie Nichols, the lad was just a cog in an industrial-scale drugs operation, and he wanted the glory of shutting it down. The fact that the operation was on his home turf was just another incentive for him; calling a halt to the racket spelled greater gravitas among his peers.

Scott hadn't had the proper incentive to find Stevie's killer, until now. And there was always the chance that hauling in the murderer might hamper his wider ambitions – make the drug traffickers more cautious and ruin his chance of the glamour collar he craved.

As I pulled up outside my parents' home I noticed the curtains twitching. I spotted Andy retreating from the window as I walked up the drive; he was standing in the hall as I walked in.

'Well?' he said.

'Well what?'

'Are there any developments?'

I didn't want to burden Andy with any more information than was necessary, the chances were it might spook him in his current frame of mind.

Tony Black

'No, Andy … all quiet on the western front.'

He retreated to the kitchen, nervously clawing at his shirt cuffs. I watched him peer into the back garden, left to right, then he started to fill the kettle. He looked distracted, weighed with thoughts, as I headed for the front room and the telephone.

I had Old Tommy's number in my wallet, next to my credit cards and an old picture of my sister's kids. The sight of Claire's nippers made my heart skip a beat as thoughts of the impending house sale rose up again.

Ringing.

He answered quickly. 'Hello …'

'Hello, Tommy.'

'Doug, long time no hear. How the hell are you, my old son?'

I skipped the pleasantries, made my request sound as businesslike as I could. Tommy knew, if I was asking at all, that it was important.

'I need to get background on a bloke called Keenan.'

The name didn't ring any bells with the RUC detective. 'Is he connected?'

'He's the first port of call for a very wayward branch of the Order we have over here.'

'And by wayward you mean …?'

I gave Tommy the abridged version of Stevie Nichols' death, of the wholesale flooding of the town with drugs.

'Sounds charming.'

I agreed. 'And folk still wonder why I'm keen to leave.'

'Moving on again, are you?'

'Making a fresh start, Tommy …' Lyn appeared in the doorway as I spoke, she waved before registering I was on a call and heading out again.

'Another fresh start, Doug?'

I smiled as Lyn left. 'A proper one this time.'

'Okay, mate ... Look, I'll see what I can dig up about this Keenan, was there anything in particular?'

I gave him the dates of Stevie Nichols' murder and asked him to check them with Keenan's movements. 'I think it was a contract hit called in from this side, but likely taken care of from Keenan's payroll.'

'I'll see what I can do, Doug.'

'I'd appreciate it, as quick as you like too, they're getting jumpy over here.'

'You know I'll do what I can.'

'Look up the line too, Tommy. I need to know who has their hand up Keenan's back.'

'I'll do my best.'

'I know you will, mate.'

I hung up.

Andy and Lyn looked pensive as I entered the kitchen. 'Everything okay, guys?'

They nodded briskly, like it was part of a shared arrangement. I thought to probe further but time was against me now.

'Okay, glad to hear it. I have to make another trip to Prestwick, to see Bert.'

Andy put down his cup. 'I'll come with you.'

I flagged him down. 'No, you stay here.' I looked towards Lyn and he seemed to get the message.

'I'll be back later, I'll be on the mobile if anyone needs me.'

Lyn got out of her seat and hugged me. 'Take care,' she said. It seemed like an overtly cautious comment; I wondered what she and Andy had been talking about in my absence.

I took the road through the town, snaking along the shore front on the beat-boy's circuit and over the John Street roundabout to Prestwick Road.

Bert Nichols was returning from a walk with his dog – a yapping Westie with a red-tartan collar – when I pulled up outside his home. He put the key in the lock and let the dog go in first. He was wiping soap smears from the bonnet of his immaculate Cavalier when I approached.

'Back again so soon?' he said.

'I hope it's convenient, Bert.'

He was too well mannered to say, 'It'll just have to be,' but his expression told a different story.

He led me through to the living room, I could hear the dog lapping at its water bowl in the back kitchen.

Bert removed his coat and sat down; he leaned forward with his elbows jutting astride his knees. I could tell from his deportment that he wasn't going to take kindly to what I had to say.

'Things have moved apace recently,' I looked him square in the eye.

No reply.

'I'm afraid you're going to have to hear some harsh truths, Mr Nichols.'

He remained impassive, seemed to sink deeper into himself. If there was a glimmer of hope in him then my words extinguished it right there.

'Bert ... I know your son was mixed up in this drugs business with Davie Grant ... and much more besides.'

He seemed to have stopped breathing, then let out a sigh and reclined further into the seat. He made an apse of his fingers above his chest as be started to speak in low decorous tones. 'I watched my son wander from the righteous path.'

It sounded like the admission a guilty man would make, not the words of a grief-stricken father.

'I know all about the split in the Order, Bert. And I need to ask you, do you think Davie Grant made the call ... to Keenan?'

The Irishman's name had little effect on Bert; he was deep in himself now, lost to the rational world. I had expected a stronger reaction, ranting maybe, but his reply shocked me.

'We're finished as an Order, now.'

'What?' I was dumbfounded. I'd just about handed him his son's killer and his first instinct was to bemoan the crumbling Order.

'Did you hear what I said, Bert? I know Keenan must have sanctioned the hit on Stevie. And Grantie's the only one who could have placed that order.'

Bert spoke softly. 'We're done for ... all those years of work, wasted.'

'Davie Grant must have instructed Keenan to kill your son, don't you see that, Bert?'

'Centuries of belief wiped out ...' He sat motionless, his pale grey eyes sunk deep in his head. I wanted to shake him by the shoulders, slap him. I needed to see that the momentous information I had delivered made some impact on him but he was near catatonic before me as he spoke, 'All those men's toil thrown on the fire.'

The sound of my ringing mobile split the air. Bert still didn't move; I reached for the phone.

'Mason ... what is it?'

'Doug, thank God you're alive.'

'*What*?'

He sounded breathless. 'I just heard the callout and I thought the worst.'

'What callout? What are you on about?'

'The emergency call ... Doug, look sorry, you obviously don't know.'

'Don't know what?'

Mason swallowed a deep breath, 'Doug, your mother's house is on fire. There's three units there now trying to put it out ... I thought the worst, I thought you were inside.'

My arm fell to my side, an enormous pressure descended on my shoulders like I was being pushed into the ground by the hand of God.

'Lyn ...'

Chapter 38

A cold wash of stolid Ayrshire sky swallowed the horizon and spat back a dark line of road. The fallow fields flew past the car in dull repetition, broken only when I passed a line of dawdling vehicles. My muscles felt slack, then tense. My fists, clamped hard to the wheel, began to squelch below the building sweat of my palms.

My mind slipped between the opposing poles of my conscience: one second begging Lyn to be alive, the next berating me for leaving her there. Andy featured lower in my thoughts, fluctuating somewhere between raw blame and downright stupidity.

I tried to weigh what might have happened, how? But my mind wanted to shuck off the burden. Nothing coherent welled in my thoughts, just glimpses of possibilities like the blurring fields and roads and cars I passed at speed. And then a black ribbon of smoke purled upwards in the distance.

As I pulled into the street the melee was everywhere. Emergency vehicles and paramedics stationed themselves like an army at war, poised and ready to meet their enemy. But the fire was gone, the house a mass of blackened walls and sunken windows that stared out like holes burned in old paper. I ran from the car towards the smouldering heap of rubble, my heart bursting in my chest.

'Lyn ...'

Suddenly, arms tight as barrel hoops latched around me.

'No, Doug ...' It was Mason.

'I need to go inside ...'

'It's not safe, Doug.'

'You don't understand ... Lyn was in there.' A siren wailed behind us, I turned to see an ambulance departing at speed. 'That's her ... she's on her way to hospital.'

I fell limply, weak. Mason released me.

'What?'

'They got her out.'

'Is she going to be okay?'

Mason's head drooped. 'I don't know, Doug.'

My mind continued to buckle under the pressure. Thoughts and images weighed in on me. I couldn't concentrate. 'But, she has to be ...'

Mason reached out a hand to steady me. 'Doug, they'll do all they can, I'm sure of it.'

A firework went off behind my eyes. 'But, what about Andy? He was in there too.'

I saw Mason's lips tighten into a thin line. 'Look, Doug ... Andy didn't make it.'

The words seemed to hit me at high speed, like I'd been flung into a wall. I couldn't recover my breath, I bent double and started to cough. Deep racking exhalations. I had smoke in my lungs now, I could feel water welling in my stinging eyes, too. Mason slapped my back, 'Come on, mate, back to the car and sit down.'

We sat in Mason's car, unmoving, silent for what seemed like an age but could only have been a few minutes.

'What happened?'

Mason stared front as he spoke, 'I don't know ... it went up very quickly.'

'Accelerant ... has to be.'

I caught him nodding to a uniform who was leaving the scene. 'We won't know till they investigate. Are you saying you have your suspicions?'

I felt my mettle returning. 'Suspicions ... Do I ever.'

Mason twisted in his seat, faced me. 'You know what you're saying, Doug?'

I knew damn well what I was saying.

'Andy was battered, worked over good and proper by Davie Grant's pugs a few days ago.'

'So what?'

'So, you think this is a coincidence, do you?'

Mason's heavy brows creased. 'I think it's a big jump from slapping someone about to murder by fire-raising.'

My head was white-hot, thoughts flashing in and out. I knew I wasn't making myself clear to him.

'Look, you don't get it. Things have moved on since we last spoke. I know Grantie's been shifting serious amounts of chemicals – Stevie Nichols was in on it too – I know Bert Nichols was against it and it nearly split the Order apart ... until a hit was called in on Stevie by a bloke called Keenan from Ulster. I know all this and you can check it out with your very own DI John Scott if you need to.'

Mason sat impassive, digesting the details I'd just served up for him. His thin lips widened momentarily and then the tip of his grey tongue flashed briefly as he tried to insinuate some moisture to allow him a reply. 'DI Scott knows about this?'

I nodded. 'You might say we've been helping each other out.'

'So, what you're telling me is that Grantie called in the hit on Stevie, and now he's singled you out for the same?'

'DI Scott had Grantie down as a suspect, Grantie hired me to try and clear his name ... I think it might have been Andy's idea, a way of wiping a debt, but now we'll never know.'

Mason wound down his window and leaned an arm on the sill. He started to light a cigarette as he spoke. 'The kicking Andy got ...'

'To call him off, or more accurately, to call me off.'

'And it didn't work, obviously.'

I took the cigarette from Mason, I felt deep guilt building in me. 'I told Andy to tell him the case would be closed when I said it was.'

Mason knew better than to turn my words back on me. He reached for his seatbelt and strapped himself in.

'Buckle up, Doug.'

'Are you taking me to the hospital?'

'Later, let the doctors do their work in peace ... Think we'll make a little visit to Mr Grant first.'

Chapter 39

As Mason turned the key in the ignition the stereo started to blare out some old-school U2. It sounded like 'Pride (in the Name of Love)' but for inexplicable reasons my mind latched onto 'The Unforgettable Fire'. I reached out and flicked the off button.

'Probably best,' said Mason. 'Not the time or place for Bono.'

There was a wisecrack in waiting somewhere, but not in my mouth. I turned to the window, watched the last of the fire crew rolling in a length of heavy hose.

On the way out to Dalmellington I found myself descending into the deepest guilt trip. I couldn't shake the image of the blackened house, the smouldering embers beneath the fallen roof. My parents' home had been destroyed, the place where Claire and I grew up; all those memories we shared from there had been scattered to the winds now.

'Oh, God ... Claire.'

'What's up?'

I scrunched my eyes tight, but the image wouldn't leave me. 'The house, I was supposed to be selling it.'

'I saw the sale board.'

'Claire didn't want me to, y'know, in the deflated market.'

Mason had the good sense to hold schtum. I spoke for us both. 'She won't have the choice now.'

As quickly as my fragile mind had alighted upon Claire and the lost house of our childhood, my thoughts changed to Andy and Lyn.

'Did you see, Lyn? I mean, before they took her away.'

Mason nodded. 'I did.'

'And ... how did she look?'

He turned to face me for a moment. 'Not good. She was unconscious, they had an oxygen mask on her.'

'But she was breathing, that's something.'

Mason carved a thin smile on the side of his face. 'Yes, that's something.'

I could tell he was choosing his words carefully. I was tempted to talk about Andy, about our shared loss of a mutual friend, but I knew that was a burden I'd have to carry alone. My friend had been killed; it seemed an unreal thought. It was only a few hours ago that I had been speaking to him. When the reality of what had happened to Andy sunk in, I knew I'd be going down with it.

As we reached Dalmellington, Davie Grant's house looked as imposing as it ever had. The one concession to the manicured garden and impressively monoblocked strip of drive was a silver-blue Cavalier, parked at an acute angle in the drive. As we pulled up I saw the driver's door of the Cavalier stood wide open, the keys were in the ignition and the engine still running.

Mason broke the silence as we stepped out. 'Strange ... looks like it's been abandoned.' He reached into the dash and removed the keys. The engine shuddered noisily then abruptly fell into silence.

The car was immaculate; it suddenly dawned on me I'd seen it before. 'I know this motor ...'

'You do?'

'It's Bert Nichols'.'

As we stood staring quizzically at each other a loud screech, like a frightened child, broke from the back of the house.

'What was that?'

Mason shrugged, jogged to the front door. It was open, we rushed through, following the increasing wails. In the corridor, just shy of the kitchen, it became clear the screaming was coming from a woman.

Mason was first through the door. As the sight of three huddled bodies greeted us we stopped still. I watched Mason take a step back, he raised his palms and tried to look non-threatening. I knew it was already too late for that when I saw the knife Bert held at a terrified Cassie's throat.

Grantie stood wide-shouldered and solid before us, he held a chubby finger out to Bert and warned him to drop the weapon. 'You've lost it, Bert ...' he yelled.

Mason ran his fingers through his hair and then returned to the open-palmed posture. 'Bert, what's going on here?'

I watched Cassie's terrified eyes widen, her short dressing gown rode up over her tanned thighs as she struggled in Bert's grip. 'Let me go ... Please, let me go.'

I stepped forward. 'Bert ... this isn't going to bring Stevie back.'

His eyes flared. 'Rubbing my nose in it, wasn't he?' His voice was a hollow dislocated rumble. He sounded nothing like the buttoned-up Bert I knew.

'What?'

'Him! He brought my son into his unholy trade.'

Grantie withdrew his finger, made a fist of his hand. There were words on his tongue but he held them back, the exertion writ-large on his red face.

'Bert ... let the girl go,' I said.

'It was a step too far, a sin in the eyes of God.'

Grantie stepped forward, pointed to me. 'I called him! I paid for his time to look at Steven's death.'

Bert bit. 'Only to clear your name, you never asked me if I wanted it.'

'They accused me and I never did it,' roared Grantie, his carotid arteries pressing out from his thick neck.

When the roaring stopped, the room fell quiet for a moment. Only Cassie's low whimpering was heard, I watched her on the tip of her toes, struggling for breath.

I spoke. 'Bert ... what's he saying?'

'He strayed far ...'

'Who?'

'My son ... he strayed from all I had taught him.'

'Bert, what are you saying?'

'It was the will of God.'

I moved closer, tried to gauge the knife's point. 'Don't you presume to judge me, Doug Michie, my actions will be judged by the Almighty alone.'

I couldn't believe what I was hearing. A fast burning fuse was lit in my gut, but the explosion occurred in my head.

'Bert, *you* called in Keenan ... you killed your own son.'

A loud roar came from deep inside Bert Nichols and he lunged back with the knife. Cassie dropped to the ground as Bert brought the blade before him. The cold steel was soundless as it seared into Davie Grant's broad chest all the way to the haft. For a second Grantie stood firm, fully aware of his fate, as he looked at the knife's handle sticking from him. He gazed up with wide, bright eyes and a slow trickle of black blood began to spill over his shirt. His mouth widened momentarily as if he was about to emit long-practiced last words into the vaults of posterity, and then he fell.

Cassie's screams sliced the still air. She knelt, keening and shaking, before her husband for only a brief spell and then, as if struck suddenly in her back, she fell onto his corpse.

Slowly, Bert Nichols turned towards myself and Mason. He took two steps towards us and then presented his wrists to Mason, as if the applying of handcuffs was the only appropriate response to the circumstance.

Epilogue

Ayr Cemetery was growing in importance to me. It seemed as if all my former attachments to the town lay there now. My father, my mother and my friend, Andy.

I stood before the small headstone and unloosened the cap on a bottle of the best Dalwhinnie.

'It's your favourite, Andy.' I said. 'Flowers didn't seem right.'

I poured half the bottle over his grave and then took a little swig for myself. 'Cheers, mate.'

I knew I would never be able to convey how I felt about Andy's death. The whole case had left me scarred in ways I never thought possible. I felt his passing was like the death of a small part of me. In many ways, I knew it was. The death of old habits, old ways, an old life.

I put down the whisky bottle and left it with my old friend. As I walked towards the car I knew it was our final parting.

The new Volvo estate was packed to the roof; the old Audi would never have held half Lyn's stuff. I knew we had to leave the Auld Toun when she told me about the call, before the fire, that Andy took.

'Doug says it's case closed when he decides ...' that's what she told me he'd said.

Andy had told her it was a call from Grantie, obviously just before he ordered the house burnt to the ground. I was less bothered about the way Grantie died when I heard that. And Cassie could do a lot of shopping with her inheritance to numb her loss.

I took the Volvo slowly through the town; for a packed car it didn't handle as sluggishly as I thought it might. The road position was higher than the Audi too, I preferred it. Maybe I was growing more attentive to safety, mine and others'.

As I drove through the town, en route back to the Horizon Hotel, I amused myself with a rough junkie count. There seemed to be fewer since I'd passed Old Tommy's findings onto DI John Scott, but I might have been mistaken. The Auld Toun had changed beyond all recognition to me, it wasn't a place I knew anymore, it was full of ghosts now.

I took the Volvo down Queen's Terrace, then onto the hotel car park. Lyn was waiting for me in the reception area as I went in.

'How are you feeling now?' I said; she still had breathing difficulties after her injuries in the fire, but the doctors said that they would pass.

'I'm fine ... raring to go, really.'

I watched as she finished up a cup of coffee, then helped her on with her coat.

'Oh, Doug ... did you get a stamp?' She pressed an envelope into my hand.

'I did, yeah.' I handed over the stamp and she passed the envelope with my sister's name and address on it to the hotel receptionist to post.

'Claire's in for a nice surprise.'

I smiled. 'A big cheque will take the sting out of recent events, I hope.'

We headed for the car, Lyn crooked her arm into mine

50 2/15

Tony Black

and leant her head on my shoulder. A weak sun broke from
the clouds as we met with the car park. The blunt silhouette
of the Isle of Arran was black against the white of the sky
and the smooth yellow of the beach, which took a rain of
blows from a ragged sea.

For the merest moment, it seemed, nothing had changed.
We were still just kids, and the Auld Toun our home.

'Still want to go?' I said.

Lyn smiled. 'Let's get out of here.'